---------- ★ ----------

"Eddie? Are you okay?"

He looked a little green around the gills.

Then she saw it, too.

A foot protruding from a green polyester pant leg. And, when she threw back the quilt, a plastic bag clinging to a square face, the color drained from it.

This isn't happening, Joan thought. It's not real.

She stooped to confirm what she already knew. Touching that foot was like touching a dressed fryer in the supermarket. Chicken under nylon.

"She's cold." Joan felt as sick as Eddie looked. "And stiff."

---------- ★ ----------

"Sara Hoskinson Frommer stitches together all the right pieces to form a warm and cozy quilt of a mystery."

—Nancy Pickard, author of
The Twenty-Seven Ingredient Chili Con Carne Mystery

D0376733

Sara
Hoskinson
Frommer

BURIED IN
Quilts

AN AUTHORS GUILD BACKINPRINT.COM EDITION

This one's for Marni

Buried In Quilts

AN AUTHORS GUILD BACKINPRINT.COM EDITION

Published by iUniverse.com, Inc.

For information address:
iUniverse.com, Inc.
5220 S 16th, Ste. 200
Lincoln, NE 68512
www.iuniverse.com

Originally published by St. Martin's

ISBN: 0-595-14306-7

Printed in the United States of America

Special thanks to Charles Brown, Peter Chase,
Doris Curran, Berniece Enyeart, George Huntington,
Kathleen McLary, Mimi Sherman, Thomas Schornhurst,
Judy Wagner, Elizabeth Warren, Dierdre Windsor,
Shelly Zegart and the Ragdale Foundation.

Author's Note

Of course this is a work of fiction. Even the place is imaginary—before naming Oliver in my first novel, *Murder in C Major,* I pored over Rand McNally maps for Indiana, Illinois, Wisconsin and Michigan, to be sure there was no such place.

"That's never Oliver, Indiana!" my mother's old friend Fannybelle wrote to her when the book came out.

"There isn't any Oliver in Indiana," I objected, sure of myself.

"Oh, yes, there is," Mom told me. "It's just a few miles from Wadesville." So much for research.

Fannybelle was right—my Oliver isn't the real Oliver, which is a tiny spot on the map published by the state. My Oliver is in Alcorn County—try finding that on a state map. But Indianapolis, Martinsville and Gnaw Bone are real.

Just as real are the traditional quilt names that head the chapters. There's only one exception: Rebecca's quilt, "After the Fall," is anything but traditional.

I've done my research this time, too, and other quilters and quilt lovers have been extraordinarily helpful. But they couldn't know what I would do with what they told me. The errors are all mine.

—Sara Hoskinson Frommer

ONE

Coffin Star

THERE WAS NO getting around it. Edna Ellett had picked
an impossible week to die.

"Not that there'd ever be a good one," Mary Sue Ellett
told Joan Spencer at Snarr's Funeral Home. "For months
we've been expecting Mother to go just any minute. But
right before the quilt show—it couldn't be worse."

Joan knew too much about grief to be shocked. But
watching Mary Sue sneak a quick look at her wrist, she
wondered why the Elletts were bothering with calling hours
at all. Surely Mary Sue didn't lack the courage to fly in the
face of local convention. She generally set her own rules—
and she wasn't shy about setting them for other people.
From all reports, she was running the twelfth annual Alcorn County Quilt Show with an iron fist.

Joan had heard plenty. She herself had no great interest
in the show. People who stroked fabric on the bolt mysti-
fied her. Needles closed their eyes to her wobbling thread,
and she had never succeeded in wearing a thimble. The
thought of cutting cloth into little pieces only to spend te-
dious hours reassembling them into one large piece, how-
ever attractive, made her want to run the other way.

So did the open coffin she faced now. Gladiolus spikes
stood watch in cardboard vases. Roses and carnations
reeked of death. Piped-in vox humana warbled it. And the
silent figure cushioned on puffy rayon in the cloth-covered

box was a poor imitation of the wiry little woman whose
fingers never had been still.

"Doesn't Edna look wonderful?" Joan heard, and
"There's something not quite right around the mouth."

How could Mary Sue bear to greet friends and strang-
ers with the shell of her mother so close by and, worse yet,
listen to them discuss Bud Snarr's embalming? Joan
wanted to scream at them.

Cremation was bad enough, she thought, remembering
the memorial services she'd lived through—first for her
mother and father and finally for her husband, who had
planned his own as if he'd known all along he wouldn't
reach forty.

Ken, a minister, had hated funerals. One bad night, after burying an old friend, he'd made Joan promise not to
put herself through such an ordeal if she outlived him.
"Wait a week or two," he'd said. "Keep it simple. And
none of those awful flowers!" It had been easy to promise—death was something far away. But then he'd col-
lapsed, leaving Joan with two children to bring up alone.

When the floral tributes had arrived by the carload, she
had sent them to nursing homes and carried armloads of
crisp lilacs from her own yard to the church. She wondered now where she'd be able to find lilacs in Oliver—and
when they'd bloom in southern Indiana. But this was
hardly the time to ask.

"I'm so sorry," she said instead, and meant it. Would
Mary Sue hear sympathy for the loss of her mother, or
only commiseration for this awkward interruption to her
busy week?

"Oh, we'll manage somehow." Mary Sue looked over
Joan's shoulder to the gathering clan.

Give her the benefit of the doubt, Joan told herself. You
don't know what she's been through, or how she handles

pain. She's more a pacer than a weeper, anyway. Sure enough, gripping Joan's arm and talking as she went, Mary Sue steered her toward the far end of the room.

"You'll want to meet the family."

Not really, Joan thought, but she let herself be swept along. She'd made herself call because Edna Ellett had been a bright spot in her work at the Senior Citizens' Center. And Mary Sue worked tirelessly on the Oliver Civic Symphony's board of directors and had a finger in who knew how many community pies. Joan was sure it was no accident that the orchestra guild had decided on a quilt raffle as one of its major fund-raising projects this year.

"My sister, Alice Franklin," Mary Sue was saying. "This is Joan Spencer, Alice. Joan works down at the old folks' center, and for the orchestra, too. She even plays—violin, isn't it?"

"Viola," Joan said automatically, recognizing in Alice a missing link between Mary Sue and their mother. A square jaw and heavy eyebrows were Edna's legacy to both her daughters, but Mary Sue, broad-shouldered and taller than Joan, would have made two of either Edna or Alice. Alice was tiny and dark. With her crowning glory coiled high on her head, she looked almost top-heavy. Her mother, too, had worn her hair in that elaborate do of women who didn't believe in cutting it—maybe they were Pentecostals. It was short now, though. Probably too hard to manage in a sickbed.

Joan marveled at hair that stayed where it was put—her own constantly threatened to escape its loose twist. Mary Sue's style was entirely different. Joan had seldom seen her in anything but polyester knit pants, with blond, frizzled permanents and overgenerous applications of eye shadow and mascara. Alice's plain gray suit, buffed nails, and sensible shoes were only to be expected in a funeral parlor, and even Mary Sue had toned down her excesses today.

"I was very sorry to hear about your mother," Joan said. "She was good to me."

"Thank you." Alice dabbed at her eyes. "It's still hard for me to believe. It all happened so fast."

"Oh? Hasn't she been sick since Christmas?"

Her diabetes had flared up then, and she'd never come back to the senior center. Joan had sent a couple of cards and phoned occasionally, but Edna hadn't always seemed sure who she was.

"Alice hasn't been home for almost two years." Mary Sue displayed her teeth. Joan knew that smile.

So, apparently, did Alice. Her eyes flashed.

"Mary Sue, I couldn't come all the way from California as often as I came up from Kentucky. Harold's just getting started out there, and everything's so expensive I can't even afford phone calls. I had no idea Mother was so bad. You didn't even tell me when she came down with the flu—I would have been here in a minute, and you knew it. It's bad enough I couldn't tell her good-bye. You make it sound as if I didn't care!"

"Now, Alice, did I say that?"

Alice didn't answer. Joan knew how she felt. Mary Sue Ellett could twist a telephone number into a personal indictment.

"Are there just the two of you?" she asked, searching for neutral ground. Edna had never mentioned a second daughter in the months before she became housebound.

"No, Alice's husband is outside, and our brother should be arriving anytime now to spell us for supper." Again Mary Sue checked her watch. "It's just like Leon to be late. We've been here since three o'clock, and my feet are killing me." She eased out of one three-inch slingback pump. Joan felt for her.

"You go ahead," Alice said. "Kitty will get me back to the house."

"I doubt it. You won't be able to pry her away from here until they lock the door tonight."

"Is Kitty another sister?" Joan asked.

"No, just a kind of shirttail cousin. Come meet her."

Mary Sue led Joan over to a slight, sad-faced woman with dark brown curls and dark circles under her eyes, drooping in one of Snarr's three wing chairs. Her head didn't reach the top of the back.

"Kitty, meet Joan Spencer," Mary Sue said. "Our cousin, Kitty Graf."

"How do you do," Joan said.

Gesturing to a wooden folding chair with "Snarr's Funeral Home" stenciled on the back, Mary Sue perched on another and slid both shoes off. Her thighs strained the polyester pants, but her feet were as dainty as Kitty's. Joan pulled the chair over and sat down. The wooden slats dug into her back.

"Kitty lived with Mother," Mary Sue was explaining.

Right. Joan remembered the day at the center when Edna had resisted when the social worker promoted an emergency phone hookup for live-alones. "I don't need that," she'd said. "I'm not alone." Joan wondered now whether Mary Sue had arranged for Kitty's presence. Her sometimes maddening efficiency often had humane results.

"That's not her up there," Kitty said flatly, ignoring Joan. "Doesn't even look like her."

"Kitty—" Mary Sue began.

"Don't tell me she's dead. I know she's dead. I was
there. She was so scared." Her eyes half-closed, Kitty
spoke to her own lap. "Now *I'm* scared."

"We'll have to put a stop to that right now!"

Joan jumped, and even Kitty looked up. The square-
jawed, bushy-browed man whose voice boomed out into
the room's solemn murmuring had to be the delinquent
Leon. He bent to kiss Mary Sue, took Kitty's hand, and
swung Alice off her feet in a bear hug.

"How're my best girls?" he asked, for all the world as
if he had come to a party. "And who's this?" He waggled
his eyebrows at Joan. "Single, I hope."

"Leon Ellett, how could you?" Two red spots stood out
on Alice's scrubbed cheeks. She smoothed her skirt and
looked down the long room toward the coffin.

"Take it easy, Alice," Mary Sue said. "Joan, my
brother Leon. Leon, this is Joan Spencer from the Senior
Citizens' Center."

"Those old ladies get better-looking every year." He
ogled her. Joan squirmed—she hoped not visibly—and
wished her brown jersey were less prone to static cling.

Alice was fuming and Kitty had withdrawn again behind the wings of her chair.

What was worrying Kitty? Her own mortality? She
couldn't be all that much older than Joan—maybe in her
fifties. The prospect of loneliness? Real grief?

Her swollen eyes met Joan's.

"I don't know what I'll do," she said. "They'll never let
me stay."

"Don't you worry about a thing," Leon boomed. "You
took care of Mom, and we'll take care of you. You'll always have a home."

Joan thought she'd hate to be a shirttail cousin, whatever that was, dependent on the Elletts.

"That old pile of stone?" Alice said, not missing a beat. "You don't want to live there all by yourself."

"Of course she doesn't." Mary Sue took over. "She just wants to stay in Oliver, don't you, Kitty? You'd rattle around in Mother's big old house, anyway. Mother wouldn't budge, but we'll find you a nice little place of your own, without all those memories."

"Edna was right," Kitty said, nodding. Her lips were tight. "She told me you'd try to push me out."

"Oh, no, Kitty," Alice protested. "We only want what's good for you."

"Well, I want the memories. I'm not moving."

Joan could have cheered. Leon did.

"Atta girl! You tell 'em."

Alice shushed him.

"For goodness' sake, Leon. Remember where you are. People are staring."

It was true. Around the room, knots of people—women Edna's age, mostly, and an occasional man—had fallen silent.

"Remember!" Leon bellowed. "I remember that when you and I were too busy for our own mother, this sweet woman stayed with her day and night. If she wants to stay there now, she's earned the right."

"Kitty, dear," Mary Sue said, showing her teeth again. "Let's talk when we're all home together. Alice and I are going back to the house now. Will you come with us, or would you rather wait with Leon?"

Joan wasn't surprised that Kitty elected to wait. She herself escaped when the Ellett sisters left. With luck, she thought, she could still manage a piece of cold chicken before the regular Wednesday orchestra rehearsal.

The cool air felt good on her face. She was on foot. It was risky to leave the car at home on a rehearsal day—her high-sounding job as an orchestra manager had turned out to involve a lot of sudden jumping to other people's beck and call. But walking was worth the risk. The mile between home and work started her blood flowing in the morning and gave her time to unwind in the evening. Besides, seven months of working among the calcium-leached bones of Oliver's senior citizens had made it abundantly clear to her that she had reason to exercise beyond burning calories. Her own back still strong and straight, Joan swung along.

She wished the distance from the funeral parlor to her little house were long enough to make the Elletts fade from her memory, as Edna seemed to have faded from theirs. Not from Kitty's, though, and she wasn't even really an Ellett. But she had lived through those final months with Edna.

Joan thought suddenly of Rebecca and wondered with a pang how distant she and her own daughter would appear to an outsider after two long years apart.

She'd have to invite Kitty to the senior center's brief memorial for Edna. Her little brass nameplate would be ready by tomorrow—the day of her funeral.

Cutting across the Oliver College campus, Joan inhaled the April dampness and concentrated on the new life vivid in the early evening light—daffodils nodding, redbud trees sprouting pink peppercorns on dark twigs, dogwood floating white against evergreens.

As her breathing became regular, her mind ran over things left undone that she ought to have done.

Practice, of course. Since she'd taken over the orchestra manager's job, she'd hardly touched her viola except on Wednesday nights, and it wasn't easy then, with all the interruptions. How had any one person ever done that whole job?

And as the orchestra's librarian, she needed to order the orchestra parts for the youth concerto competition winner's piece on the spring concert. Jennifer Werner, daughter of the professor in whose laboratory Joan's son, Andrew, worked several hours a week, had won it with a Vivaldi oboe concerto. Jennifer had flourished ever since she had been asked last fall to play as a regular member of the orchestra after the murder of the first oboist. Not many high school kids could have stepped in so quickly, but Jennifer had carried it off. Andrew had been right about her.

He met Joan at the door, gnawing on a drumstick.

"Mom, you just missed the phone."

Probably someone calling to beg off rehearsal. It happened every Wednesday.

"Who's not coming tonight?" Joan dumped her shoulder bag on the sofa. Small as it was, she knew the Oliver Civic Symphony could rehearse minus a fiddle or two.

Andrew followed her into the kitchen.

"Mom, it was Rebecca."

"Is she all right? Andrew, what did she say?" Joan held her breath. Rebecca hadn't called or written since last summer, before they had moved to Oliver. At Christmas, she had signed a store-bought card—Rebecca, who always took pride in making her own. At first, Joan had reassured herself that Rebecca was busy, if perhaps struggling. But the reassurance was long gone.

"She didn't say much," Andrew answered. "I think she wants to come home." He always had been able to read between his sister's lines. He'd missed her since she'd left home at eighteen. Almost two years ago.

"What did you tell her? Did you get her number?"

"I asked, but she just said she'd call back. I didn't know where you were."

"And I won't be home again until after ten. Of course she can come. I just hope nothing's happened."

"I promised Mr. Werner I'd work at the lab. You think I should stay home?"

Joan hesitated only a moment.

"No, you go ahead. Maybe she'll call before I have to leave. Have you had supper?"

"Yep." Andrew flipped the clean bone into the garbage and licked his fingers.

"Good. If I eat fast, I'll just about make it." She stuck her head into the refrigerator, trying to think about food. "Where's the rest of the chicken?"

"Um—" His eyes swung toward the garbage. "You had plans for it?"

"Andrew Spencer! You didn't eat that whole roaster!"

"It wasn't whole. More like half."

At seventeen, Andrew had already reached his father's height, and he showed no sign of stopping. Some days she despaired of filling him.

"Guess I'll have to settle for yogurt."

"Sorry, Mom." He wasn't, really, and neither was she. "I'll see you later, okay?" He reached for the doorknob.

"Okay," she said, and he was out the back door, untethering his ten-speed and hoisting it over the back-porch railing. "Did you fix your bike light?" she called after him. Suddenly deaf, he swung one long leg over the crossbar and disappeared around the corner of the house.

Joan dawdled until she could put it off no longer. She rinsed her bowl and spoon, collected her viola and the box of music folders, shouldered her bag, turned on the porch light, and locked the door.

Halfway down the front walk, she heard the telephone.

TWO

Follow-the-Leader

IN THE END, she was late.

Ordinarily, Alex Campbell conducted without apparent concern for her players' time. Ordinarily, Joan arrived well ahead of time to consult with her, distribute new music or the folders of players who hadn't taken theirs home to practice, and make general announcements while the last few people straggled in.

Tonight nothing was ordinary.

After parking in the fire lane to avoid a ten-minute trek to the auditorium past the cars and school buses that crowded the Oliver Consolidated High School parking lot (some school function must be going on, she thought) Joan sprinted down the long hall. The corners of the music box poked her left calf as she ran, and the weight of the viola pulling on her bow arm made her wish, not for the first time, that she'd never let herself be talked out of playing the flute.

"There she is!" The shout went up as soon as she opened the auditorium door.

"Where have you been?" Alex demanded with the force she usually reserved for a player who missed a cue in dress rehearsal. "You know we don't have this kind of time to waste. We play in a week."

Joan's cheeks burned. She hurried to the back of the stage and dumped her things on the table from which refreshments would be served during the break. Unstrap-

ping the box, she distributed folders to players who circled
it like moths around a light.

This is ridiculous, she thought. They should have been
able to start without me. A week away from the concert I
shouldn't be taking home anything but extra parts. Isn't
anyone practicing?

By the time she could slide into fourth chair of the viola
section, Alex was already announcing the two dances from
Aaron Copland's ballet *Rodeo*—"Saturday Night Waltz"
and "Hoedown."

There were, Joan thought, worse pieces to begin on if
you hadn't had a chance to tune. During the bars that
mimicked a fiddler tuning up, she listened for the open A
and checked her own four strings. Then came the waltz it-
self, sweet and slow. Back to the open strings, and the
"Hoedown" cut loose—a joy, with notes that fell comfortably under her fingers and bowing that rollicked over
the strings as if there could be no other way. First down
low in comfortable viola range—then much faster and
higher, but still delightfully playable. The violas even had
the tune!

For years now, Joan had preferred her awkwardly large
instrument above all others, even when her back ached
from supporting it. She loved its warm sound enough not
to mind the cracks people made about violists as incom-
petent violinists demoted to playing easy parts: "What do
musicians call a half step?" "Two viola players trying to
play the same note." And she knew all too well why playing second fiddle meant standing in someone's shadow—
the first violins got all the good tunes. But compared to the
violas, even the seconds basked in sunshine. What would
it be like to play the melody like this all the time?

John Hocking, her stand partner, was digging in with
enthusiasm. His jaw tucked into his chin rest, he gave her

a lopsided grin when she leaned forward to turn the last page.

The rehearsals had gone well over the past several weeks, and this relaxed fun was the payoff.

Even Alex found little to criticize.

"If you can do that in the concert, we'll have them all dancing," she said. "Let's run through the fanfare. You strings be patient a minute—I'll need you for the Ives before the break."

Joan had learned enough about Alex's "minutes" not to face them without something to stave off boredom. She'd spend this one checking the orchestra personnel list for errors before taking the program to the printer. She wished she'd paid closer attention to that whole process last fall, when Yoichi Nakamura was manager. She hadn't known then that she would inherit his job, or how impossible some of the simplest things could be. Like getting the orchestra members to correct their names before it was too late.

"Are you all right?" John Hocking asked softly when she laid her viola on her seat and turned back to the table where she'd left the list. "It's not like you to be late."

"I'm fine," she said, and for the moment, she was. Then the worry swept over her again—worry that had made her, late or not, incapable of ignoring what had surely been Rebecca's call. But her front-door key had jammed in the lock, she'd fumbled the receiver, and finally only the dial tone had rung in her ear.

John had a daughter—he'd understand. But what could she say, even to him? My daughter's in trouble? She didn't know any such thing.

A hush behind her meant that Alex had lifted her baton. Staring into the raised bells of the brass section, Joan knew it was time to move while she still had all her hearing. She'd often wished for one of those clear plastic baffles some orchestras attached to the back of a chair to protect the ears of the player sitting in it from unbearable volume close behind. Now she just scooted past John and behind the brass. From back there, she quite liked Copland's "Fanfare for the Common Man," with which the concert would begin. There were some compensations to being manager, she thought. Alex would have fussed if another player had taken an unauthorized break, but everybody expected her to move around during rehearsal.

Her problem was getting in enough playing time. She was forever hopping up to deal with some interruption or other. She hadn't yet played through Ives's "Unanswered Questions," and it worried her.

It was the scoring—for strings, flutes, and solo trumpet—that had done her in. In a rare instance of sensible scheduling, Alex had been saving the piece for the end of each week's rehearsal, to let the rest of the orchestra go home. Between checking out music and hearing players' complaints, Joan hadn't yet managed to rehearse it. And unlike much of the raucous music of Charles Ives, this brief piece was so soft that she didn't even know how her part sounded. She was glad Alex had decided to tack it on to the first half of the rehearsal tonight. The others could take an extra-long break instead of leaving early.

When the last notes of the fanfare sounded, she put away her lists and programs, went back to the table, picked up her viola, and tightened her bow.

"I'll be out of your way now," she said to the new volunteer from the symphony guild who had begun setting out cups and cookies for the break. "Where's your help?" Usually those ladies came in pairs, like Mormon missionaries.

"Mary Sue Ellett was scheduled, but you know her mother died, so of course she won't be here," the woman said. "I don't mind doing it alone. It's no trouble."

Well, no. Joan had long suspected the orchestra members of being capable of ladling their own punch. But someone had baked those cookies at home.

"Thank you," she said, her managerial hat on firmly. "We really appreciate all the guild does for the orchestra." Resisting temptation, she started back to her seat to play the Ives at last.

She should have known.

"Joan! I have to talk to you!" Mary Sue Ellett was squeezing her way between the stands. The players hunched protectively over their instruments as she descended on them, and the glare Alex directed at her back would have shriveled a tuba.

"Would you believe that?" the guild volunteer asked nobody in particular. "Her own mother!"

Good thing you didn't see her at the funeral parlor, Joan thought. She intercepted Mary Sue as she emerged from between the violas and woodwinds.

"Let's go out in the hall," Joan said. "They're about to start the Ives."

"Ives—good Lord, yes. We wouldn't be able to hear ourselves think."

In the echoing, chairless hall, the tiled floor stretched uninvitingly, streaked with spring mud from hundreds of young feet. They stood—Joan comfortably flat, Mary Sue teetering over her in the spike heels she'd worn to the calling hours at Snarr's.

What could be so important that she'd come here tonight? Joan wondered.

"You have to help me."

Mary Sue always was one for coming right to the point without saying anything.

"How?"

In the past few months, Joan had learned not to say yes too soon. After the scene she'd witnessed at Snarr's, she wasn't inclined to say much of anything.

"I want to talk to the orchestra. It's about the quilt show you're playing for."

Joan hadn't thought of it quite that way. The Oliver College Fine Arts Department, the Oliver Quilters' Guild, and the Alcorn County Historical Society had indeed asked the orchestra to play this all-American concert during the week of the quilt show, as a kind of added attraction. With Mary Sue representing the guild on the symphony board, the question had been settled quickly. The concert, like the show, would take place in the historic Sagamore Inn.

"What about it?" Joan asked now.

"I'm short ten sitters. The orchestra will just have to fill in—I'm running out of time."

"The orchestra—" Joan stopped dead. "Mary Sue, these people love music, and they'll play for a quilt show or almost anything else that's legal. But they don't do babies." Or windows.

"No, no, no. Not baby-sitters. Hall sitters—to watch over the quilts. I talked to your friend Lieutenant Lundquist. He's in charge of security, and he was sure you'd help." Mary Sue showed white teeth between startlingly red lips. She'd touched up her makeup since leaving Snarr's. "He'll be disappointed in you, Joan."

Oh, the joys of living in a small town. In Mary Sue's mouth, "your friend" sounded serious. Actually, Joan hadn't seen Fred Lundquist for months, but quilts weren't the only things created out of whole cloth in Oliver. She knew Fred well enough, though, to be morally certain that he wouldn't have volunteered her to do anything without asking first.

On the other hand, why should she be caught in the middle? The players could speak for themselves. Maybe some would even want to help.

"You ask them, Mary Sue. Quilting's not my thing." Neither is extortion.

"I'm sorry, Joan. Of course." The battle won, Mary Sue could afford to be gracious. "Will you at least introduce me?"

"Oh, sure. Come on."

They went back in to hear the last plaintive trumpet theme trail off. The strings faded away to nothing and then less than nothing, bows scarcely moving, only a few hairs touching. Alex stood with her eyes almost closed, the baton pointing to her chin and a finger to her lips. Then she dropped her hands and smiled, her round face lighting up.

"Nice job, all of you. For the concert, we'll have the strings in the wings, the flutes up here, and the trumpet— Joan, would you see if we can put him in the balcony? That would be ideal."

Joan waved agreement and went forward.

"Before you break, Alex, we have a couple of announcements."

"Let's keep it short. We started late," Alex said, but she stepped down with what looked like relief, fanning herself with one pudgy hand and heading around the cellos toward the iced punch.

Joan stood by the podium.

"Be sure to check how your name is spelled on the personnel list by the door. What's on that list is what goes on the program. The concert will be a week from Sunday in the ballroom of the old Sagamore Inn. We'll rehearse there next Wednesday.''

''What about music stands?'' someone called from the back.

''Bring stands. Concert dress is the usual long black. That's it from me. Now Mary Sue Ellett, from the guild, has a favor to ask. Then we'll break, but you heard Alex. Five minutes.''

Joan waved Mary Sue forward and wandered back to the punch and cookies. The guild volunteer, her mouth open and her eyes on Mary Sue, handed Joan a cup. Never retiring, Mary Sue mounted the podium.

''You sounded beautiful just now,'' she began.

How would she know? Joan thought. She didn't hear more than fifteen seconds of it. And I'm not going to listen to that much of *her*. Lifting a cookie from the plate, she ducked out.

THREE

Merry-Go-Round

LIEUTENANT FRED LUNDQUIST, OPD, was already covered up when Captain Altschuler dropped the quilt show on him. All year, a rash of overnight computer thefts had been plaguing college offices. Rather than lugging off heavy printers or bulky monitors, the thief or thieves were breaking into the machines to steal only the expensive chips and cards that made them run. Months of hard work had disappeared with the hard disk drives on which it was stored. Thousands of dollars' worth of such stolen goods could be concealed in an instant, leaving the police few options. Asking every person moving on campus at night to strip to the buff was not one of them.

Just once, they'd come close. Late one evening, a professor returning to finish writing an exam had chased a man he saw leaving his office. Yelling, he attracted the attention of a police officer patrolling the campus. The man escaped over a seven-foot chain-link fence, leaving bits of a brown cotton shirt and old blue jeans on its prongs. The professor couldn't tell them much except that he was tall.

"And in some kind of shape! He went over that fence as easily as I'd walk upstairs."

A student? Maybe. Maybe not. The professor, not given to backing up his hard drive on floppy disks, had left the station house mourning the loss of at least a month's work—and his database of old exam questions.

Spring break, when many faculty members and most students alike skipped town, would leave the computers on campus even more vulnerable than usual, and Fred knew it would increase the ordinary sort of burglaries in houses and dorms. And the annual influx of visitors to the quilt show would attract con artists and purse snatchers and give them crowds in which to disappear. It happened every year.

THROUGH HIS OPEN office door, Fred could see the woman berating Kyle Pruitt. He thought he might have heard her even if the oak door had been closed.

"Laundry!" she exploded. "Just because it was hanging outside doesn't make it laundry! If you don't appreciate the value of art, take me to someone who does!"

Fred couldn't see Kyle or hear his reply, but he could imagine the color spreading across the freckled face. Assertive women flustered Sergeant Pruitt. Angry ones did him in. Fred wondered how long he would hold out.

She towered over Pruitt in a camouflage jacket and farmyard boots, with a flowing skirt that almost touched the boots. Her dark hair, streaked with what had to be premature gray, was on the wild side, but even in her anger her vowels were shaped and her consonants precise.

Not from around here, Fred thought. Another East Coast dropout. Living in the cooperative, maybe, or trying to eke out a living with a garden and a cow. She probably ought to be ranting in the sheriff's office, not the OPD. Wonder how long she'll last. She's made it through the winter, anyhow.

He couldn't hear Pruitt's soft reply.

"No, I won't sit down, and don't give me that 'boys will be boys' crap," the woman raged. "You haven't done a thing for two weeks—I won't let you put me off any longer.

This isn't vandalism, it's theft! That quilt was unique. I dyed and printed the cloth myself. It stood a good chance of winning the top prize next week. Now I've missed the deadline. Your 'boys' have done me out of at least five thousand.''

Maybe, Fred thought. But I hear the competition's pretty stiff.

"You get your act together and find out who took my quilt," she said. "Or what you're calling a prank will cost Oliver one hell of a lot more than it cost me. I don't have to go to court, either. If I get the word out, the quilters will boycott your precious show. Nobody's going to send good work to a rinky-dink town where the cops treat a valuable quilt like a pair of coed's panties."

Boycott? Never mind jurisdiction. It was time to get involved. Fred picked up his phone and dialed Pruitt's extension.

"Come on in, Kyle," he said. "And bring her with you. Let's see what we can do."

"SOMETHING MORE your size, Fred," Captain Warren Altschuler had called the request from the Alcorn County Quilt Show committee earlier in the week.

Fred had quirked a blond eyebrow and smiled down at the stocky chief of detectives standing in his office door.

"Thimbles?"

"This is serious. I wouldn't lie to you." Warren Altschuler's pug-ugly face was as earnest as his gravelly voice.

It was true. Since his success in solving last fall's orchestra murders, Fred had been treated with noticeably greater respect. There was no point in thinking about a promotion or raise until the Oliver town council passed the budget in June, but for a few months he'd been getting decent assignments. He no longer daydreamed of retiring.

"Sorry," he said, and meant it. "Take a load off. What's their problem?"

For years the quilt show had managed without an official police liaison. Just off the courthouse square, the grand old Sagamore Inn was spitting distance from the police department—an officer or the ambulance could be there at a moment's notice.

Altschuler chose a straight wooden chair instead of the big old leather one he usually preferred. Fred cleared a corner of his desk for Altschuler's feet and settled his big Swedish frame in the swivel chair behind it, but Altschuler kept his feet on the floor.

"Theft. Big stuff."

"Since when?" Fred couldn't remember a serious incident at the show in his years in Oliver. There might be a call or two about someone overcome by the heat in the historic building, authentic to its lack of air-conditioning—and indoor plumbing, for that matter. He was grateful that the purists had weakened on the matter of electricity.

"So far we've been lucky," Altschuler said. "But the quilters' guilds are boycotting shows where quilts walked off last year. One up in Indy closed before it opened."

No wonder they're panicking, Fred thought. It wouldn't make a dent in the economy of a city the size of Indianapolis, but here . . .

The quilt show was to Oliver what the football season was to towns with bigger, more sports-minded colleges. It brought in so much outside money that the owner of the restaurant half a block from the historic inn didn't even blink when visitors paraded into his spotless rest rooms without ordering. For a couple of weeks each year the show provided all the customers he could serve. Oliver's row of antique and gift shops flourished, the downtown hotel was booked solid, the OliveRest Motel's VACANCY sign sprouted a seldom-used NO, and all the gas stations jacked up their prices.

With Fine Arts cosponsoring the show, Oliver College cleared a welcome profit by renting out dormitory rooms vacated for spring break. Grumbling all the while about the inconvenience, students locked up their stereos and cleaned house in exchange for a discount on their second-semester room rates.

Fred stretched back, lacing his fingers into a cushion for his head and anchoring his toes under a desk drawer to protect his fingers from crashing into the shelf behind him when he leaned too far. He and the old swivel chair had reached a truce of sorts.

"Just what do they want?" he asked.

"What they want is one thing." Altschuler grinned suddenly and tapped the desk. "What they get is you. I don't care how you make them like it, as long as you don't foul up the duty roster. Plug holes in their security with their people, not ours." The grin disappeared. "But plug 'em."

"Any idea how they run things?"

"Nope. I steer clear. Last year Janice was after me to spend a thousand dollars for a quilt you couldn't even sleep under. Can you believe that? She was going to hang it behind the couch." He shook his head. "I stopped that in a hurry. She didn't speak to me for a week."

Fred nodded that he was listening, his face carefully neutral. He'd been through enough Altschuler family wars to know that safety lay in silence. If Linda Lundquist had been the spendthrift Janice Altschuler was, maybe he'd have dumped her, instead of the other way around. Fred, not Linda, had been the one who put money into their house. He'd thought of it as protecting his investment. In the end, of course, it was Linda's house—and Linda's capital gains when she left town. And Warren Altschuler, though not a friend, had seen him through the worst of it.

Altschuler sighed.

"Mary Sue Ellett's running things," he said. "Good luck."

LATER, FRED WONDERED whether the Romans had wished the Christians luck before throwing them to the lions. He thought it would have done about as much good.

The committee's security arrangements weren't bad. Only the front door of the Sagamore Inn was to be open to the public. Small items—patterns, books and videos on quilting, scissors and rotary cutters, quilting templates, thread, beeswax, and special leather thimbles—would be sold in the ordinary way during the show, but any quilts sold were to be left on display with the rest until the last day, with red dots stuck beside their listed prices. Only then, on receipt of an official claim check, would a committee member bring each quilt out to its owner at a table blocking the entrance to the first display room.

At the heart of the system was the "hall sitter," someone dragooned into spending long hours watching people, quilts, and the other doors. At night all the doors could be locked and a guard posted, but in the daytime the fire marshal's rules required that all doors open from the inside.

"The side and back doors represent the greatest threat," Fred said. "You can't tuck something as big as a quilt under your coat and fake your way past the desk at the front, but it wouldn't be hard to skip out the side if no one's near."

A withering look from Mary Sue Ellett told him how original that thought was.

Traditionally, Fred learned, rubber stamps took the place of tickets, with a different patch stamped on the visitors' hands each day. Committee members, judges, lecturers, and commercial exhibitors would be issued photo ID cards.

He volunteered the department's Polaroid. Mary Sue put her foot down.

"I will not drag our distinguished authorities into the police station for a mug shot. Besides, the license branch camera turns them out with a plastic coating." So does ours, Fred thought.

"For a fee," one committee member objected. "I think we should seriously consider the lieutenant's offer. Why throw money away?"

"The police station's closer, too," said another.

"We've always used the license branch," said Mary Sue. And it was settled.

Fred didn't take it personally. He suspected that Mary Sue's distinguished authorities were in for a rude awakening.

He sat back while they discussed procedures for hanging the show. Only the police, the president of the historical society, the chair of the Oliver College Fine Arts Department, and Mary Sue would have keys to the building.

"We'll do most of the work Tuesday and Wednesday," she said. "Wednesday night the orchestra is coming in for a rehearsal, and the judges and lecturers will preview the show. Judging will start Thursday. I don't know yet when the Amish quilts will arrive from the state museum. If they come late, we're going to need some last-minute help. At least they're coming. We're still on tenterhooks about that wonderful Susan McCord vine quilt from the Henry Ford Museum."

"I thought that was a sure thing," said a young man with a beard whom Fred didn't know.

"They were sympathetic because she was a Hoosier. But then they heard we were in a historic building. They don't just want security and a glass case. They may insist on total climate control."

"Can't be done," the man said.

"I know," said Mary Sue. "So we'll have to be flexible. I've saved one whole room for it. If we're turned down at the last minute, I have something else in mind."

At the end of the meeting, Fred came back to the all-important watchers.

"I take it that you already have your roster of hall sitters?"

"If we did, I'd sleep easier," Mary Sue said. "We're only two weeks away. I didn't get any cooperation to speak of from the orchestra, even though we're doing a major fund-raiser for them. The manager wouldn't even ask them for me; I had to do it myself."

Fred hid a smile at the image of Joan Spencer standing up to Mary Sue Ellett. He remembered her as warm and appealing, but she'd certainly held her own last fall when he was suspecting her friends in the orchestra.

Now, FACED WITH someone who clearly would have no trouble confronting anyone, he thought he saw a way to solve two problems in one.

"Miss—?" he asked.

"Carolyn Ryrie," the woman said. "And it's Ms."

"Lieutenant Lundquist, Ms. Ryrie." They shook hands. "We'll do our best to find your property. How much would you say it's worth? Not its potential winnings, you understand, but a sale price?"

"It's listed at three thousand dollars."

"Then we're talking about felony theft, which we take very seriously. I'm working closely with the organizers of the quilt show, and I'm sure I can promise you some expert help in tracking down your missing quilt—in addition, of course, to what we can do."

"Well," she said, and for the first time he could see the attractive woman behind the anger.

"I think they'd be even more inclined to help if you could see your way clear to volunteering some time next week to watching the quilts on display. They're at risk, too. And if you think you recognize someone who might have taken yours, we can be there in no time."

She thawed. Smiled.

"I was going to the show anyway," she said. "Sure, Lieutenant, I'll do it. And thanks."

"Sergeant Pruitt," Fred said.

"Yessir?" Kyle had been standing back, probably hoping to be forgotten. Not for the first time, Fred wondered how he'd ever made sergeant.

"Get a description of Ms. Ryrie's missing quilt—a photograph, if she has one—and any information she can give us about its disappearance."

"Yessir."

FOUR

Mother's Delight

REBECCA SOUNDED a long way away. The distance between them crackled in Joan's ear.

"Mom, did I wake you?"

"Rebecca! No, it's fine. I'm just getting dressed." Joan smiled into the receiver. "It's so good to hear you."

"What time is it in Indiana, anyway?"

"Seven-thirty. Do you want me to call you back?"

Sitting on the edge of the bed in her slip, only one leg into her panty hose, she fumbled for the pencil and pad on the bookcase headboard.

"That's okay." Rebecca wasn't giving anything away. Same old Rebecca. Or was she?

"Are you all right?"

"Mother, of course I'm all right." Of course, Joan thought. You're not quite twenty, you're on your own, your old telephone was disconnected, you haven't answered a letter for months—what could possibly be wrong? She fought back the sarcasm and tried to inhale the relief.

"Andrew said you called last night."

"I tried again," Rebecca said. "But nobody answered."

"I was already outside. I couldn't unlock the door in time."

"You seeing somebody, or what?"

The words were adult, but the child came through loud and clear. Rebecca had loved her father as fiercely as she had resented her fishbowl life as a preacher's kid. She had made it abundantly plain to Joan that no one else could ever possibly live up to him. After his death, more than one man had backed away from the girl with the stony face—and her mother.

"I was on my way to work."

"At night?"

"Orchestra night. I wrote you about the orchestra."

Rebecca could spar like this all day, Joan knew. Shutting her mind to the clock and resisting the temptation to hurry things along, she leaned her ear into the receiver and snaked her left leg into the bunched-up nylon.

The wait was mercifully brief.

"Mom, do you think you could put me up for a while?"

Andrew had been right.

"Of course!" Joan concentrated on the smile she wanted Rebecca to hear. "That's wonderful. When are you coming?"

"Next week. I've entered the Oliver quilt competition. It's only one of the most prestigious small shows in the whole country."

"It is?"

"You mean you didn't *know?*"

Ignorant about quilts and quilting, Joan hadn't known that anyone outside southern Indiana was likely to care what happened in Oliver. Nor had she ever known Rebecca to show the slightest interest in anything domestic.

"All I know is that the symphony's going to play for it."

"Well, that ought to give you an idea, right there."

What it gave her was a headache and a mental image of Mary Sue Ellett in charge of an even grander wingding than she'd suspected.

"Mom . . ." Rebecca began, and stopped.

"Mmm?"

"You...you won't get in my way while I'm there, will you?"

Joan took a deep breath and tried the obvious.

"It's a little house, Rebecca. We'll probably trip over each other."

"You know what I mean," Rebecca said. "I don't want you asking me where I'm going, and when I'm coming in, and...and bothering me."

"Don't worry." Joan's sense of humor came to the rescue. "I won't bother you if you won't bother me."

"You *are* seeing someone."

The worst of it, Joan thought after they hung up, was that it wasn't true. Even without Rebecca to scare them off, the few eligible men she'd met in Oliver were keeping their distance. It would be a shame to put up with all that suspicion for nothing. She'd have to invite Fred Lundquist over. She wondered what Rebecca would say to a police detective.

She wondered, for that matter, what Rebecca would say about anything. Rebecca had left home so young, unwilling to accept any advice, determined to make her way in the world armed only with a high school diploma and her own talents. Joan understood her need to separate, but she wished Rebecca weren't so all-fired stubborn about her independence. Somehow, though, her vulnerable daughter had landed on her feet, at least at first. She'd found a place to live and some kind of job at a bank where one of her housemates worked. Two years later, that was all Joan knew about it. She hoped they were treating her right—the disconnected phone suggested money problems Rebecca wouldn't want to admit to her.

Rushing now, she pulled Tuesday's gray skirt and her favorite red cable sweater over a fresh blouse and gave her mostly brown hair half a dozen hard brush strokes before skewering it into a loose twist. She laced her feet into gray Hushpuppies and ran downstairs to the kitchen.

By the time she left the house she was humming.

THE ELLETTS didn't come to the Senior Citizens' Center that afternoon, but the shirttail cousin did. Kitty Graf quietly performed the honors on a step stool—some tall person with scant common sense had hung the carved memorial board too high for most of the little old regulars. Now Edna's nameplate shone in the late-afternoon sun below that of Elmer Rush, briefly the orchestra's first bassoonist, who had died suddenly only a few months earlier.

Joan wondered which of the old people would be next. She was thankful that the memorial was brief.

"We just want to remember," Annie Jordan had told her on one of her first days at work. "Some like to sing. I'll tell you, though—anybody caterwauls over me when my time comes, I'll come back to haunt 'em."

Joan hoped Annie's time was a long way off. She had come to love this plainspoken old woman.

Shaking hands with Edna's old friends, Kitty looked less forlorn than she had at Snarr's. The circles under her eyes were still there, though. Small wonder, Joan thought. She's stuck with the Elletts.

Kitty caught her eye and Joan went over to her.

"Would you mind coming out to the car?" Kitty asked. "I'm supposed to give you a quilt."

"Why me?" But Joan followed her out into the sunshine.

"It's the one the orchestra guild made. Edna was too sick to quilt with them, but Mary Sue volunteered her to do the edges and hem the binding. She managed a little."

Kitty pulled the sheet-wrapped bundle from the back seat of an ancient Buick.

Joan took it but wondered what on earth to do with it.

"Mary Sue said you'd get someone here to finish it off," Kitty added.

It's not enough to want the orchestra to quilt-sit, Joan thought. But at least she asked them herself. Now she's really dumping on me.

Joan's face must have given her away. Kitty reached for the bundle.

"You didn't know? Never mind. Maybe I can help." Sudden tears made her eyes bright. "I have time now."

Joan hugged the quilt.

"Kitty, I don't know the first thing about quilts. But it's true that we're planning to raise money with this one. I guess it's part of my job—my other job. And someone here might be able to finish it. Don't worry about it."

"I wouldn't mind. Really. Edna quilted most of it before she got so bad."

"You're sure?" Joan was grateful. "I'll ask at the center, but we may have to take you up on that. There's not much time left."

AT FIVE, when the center's board of directors gathered, Edna Ellett's death headed the unspoken agenda.

"I still can't believe it," said Annie Jordan, knitting without watching. Like Edna, she couldn't bear to sit idle—and she didn't count mere meetings as work. "Last week she looked pretty good. She was in bed, but she said she felt all right."

"You saw her?" asked Margaret Duffy, who had been Joan's sixth-grade teacher when her father had spent a sabbatical year at Oliver College, and who had recommended her to the board when she'd arrived in Oliver last year without a job. Margaret's hands lay folded over her ample middle.

"I saw her most weeks," Annie said. "If I couldn't stop by, I'd call. I'm about the only one who did. That crew at her house this week probably won't recognize half the things they're picking over." Her fingers flicked the yarn.

"Leon certainly won't—not that he'll care," said Margaret. "He's feathered his nest without any help from his mother. I imagine those girls are at it tooth and nail over Edna's pie safe and cherry corner cupboard. Not to mention her quilts."

"Alice doesn't know a quilt from a comfort," Annie said.

"That's never stopped her," said Margaret. "Last time she came up from Kentucky before she moved out west, she decided Edna's wildflower garden was a weed patch and had a man with a Rototiller over there burying maidenhair fern and lady slippers. Edna had managed to get them to grow in town. Trust Alice not to ask."

Margaret would know, Joan thought. She'd probably taught the Elletts in school.

"Alice was stubborn as a child," Margaret went on as if she'd read Joan's mind. "She never let facts get in her way. She just talked her husband into moving to California to get rich, and now she's stuck there—they can't afford to move back to Kentucky. Mary Sue's the practical one."

"Mary Sue, she knows quilts, anyway," Annie conceded. "She was always pushing Edna to let her show them, but Edna never would. She had some old ones—real special—and dealers and museums breathing down her neck. Now Mary Sue can haul out all the antiques. She'll let Alice think she's getting the best, but she'll glom on to anything that matters for herself."

"Mary Sue deserves something," Margaret said quietly. "She made sure Edna had what she needed."

Lowering her eyes to her knitting for the first time, Annie stuck one needle in her topknot and slid pairs of stitches along the other, tightening her lips as if counting. Joan couldn't see anything in the plain sock to count.

"Things, maybe," Annie finally squeezed out. "I expect Mary Sue carried in groceries a time or two. Mainly she just fixed it for Kitty to come live there. Kitty's the one who did for Edna. And you know how much *she'll* get."

Alvin Hannauer, a retired anthropologist with whom Joan's father had worked, looked up over his wire-rims. "Edna was a fair woman. And she left a will, I know."

Annie shook her head. "By the time they get to a will, anything worth wanting is gone. If the kids don't sneak it out, the neighbors do. I know for a fact that my Aunt Goldie's silver candlesticks walked off before she was in her grave. I could tell you where, if I had a mind to."

Joan was relieved when Alvin called the meeting to order. As usual, he handled routine matters with dispatch. Then he unfolded a letter.

"We've had a request for volunteers this week," he said. "From the symphony."

"I'm not stuffing any more envelopes," said Annie. "Folks think that's all we're good for."

"Don't get your back up, Annie," Alvin said mildly. "You haven't heard what they want yet."

Annie subsided, but her knitting picked up speed.

"It's for next week's quilt show."

"I'm not baby-sitting quilts, either."

"Okay, Annie," Alvin said. "But some people like to."

"What does the orchestra want, Joan?" Annie asked.

"The orchestra," Alvin said, staring her down, "or the orchestra guild, to be precise, has made a musical quilt as a fund-raiser. They want a crack at the out-of-town money, too. It's all but finished, and they're asking for volunteers to do the edges in time for the show."

"She took her time asking," Annie grumped.

The letter had eased Joan's earlier resentment. Now, torn between her loyalties to the center and the orchestra, she felt obliged to clear the air.

"I can tell you a little about this," she said. "Edna Ellett was going to bind it for Mary Sue, but of course she couldn't. As a matter of fact, the quilt's already here. Kitty Graf brought it over this afternoon and volunteered to work on it. If someone will show me, maybe even I can learn how."

I can't believe I said that, she thought. But it worked. Mabel Dunn, who took the minutes and seldom said anything, spoke now.

"I'll help. And I'll teach you. I'm not great shakes, but there's nothing to binding a quilt. Seems as if it's as much for Edna as it is for the orchestra."

"Thanks, Mabel," Alvin said. "Without objection, then, I'll ask Joan to post the letter on the bulletin board downstairs. And without objection, the meeting stands adjourned."

Past worrying about Mary Sue's sensibilities, Joan called her to insist on help recruiting volunteers.

"You can't just spring jobs on me like this," she said. "Not only am I busy here, but there's still lots to do for the orchestra before the concert. The people who thought this project up need to see it through."

They finally agreed on a time—Friday after lunch, when the big room at the center would be free.

That was probably a waste of breath, Joan thought after she hung up. But it was worth it. If all else fails, Mabel Dunn and Kitty Graf will come. I'd better let them know when.

FIVE

Hands All Around

THE FIRST TO ARRIVE on Friday was a stranger. Joan was sure she'd met all the orchestra guild members. The young woman standing in her office door with a skirt that met her unfashionable boots wasn't one of them.

"I'm Carolyn Ryrie," she said. "They told me you needed quilters this afternoon."

"Bless you," Joan said. "Who told you?"

"The woman's name is Ellett, but I suppose you could say the police sent me. It's a long story."

The story had to wait, though. Mabel Dunn and Kitty Graf were already there. Joan introduced them, told Kitty where to find the quilt, and excused herself to check the tables they'd work around.

Opening the door to the activity room, she inhaled chicken and dumplings. Since she had come to the center in September, the occasional carry-in lunch had been replaced by a government-sponsored nutrition program for the elderly. Those who could were asked to pay $1.50 a meal. Everyone was encouraged to contribute at least something, but no one was turned away. Annie Jordan called it "eats for old folks."

Occasionally, when meat loaf with onion permeated the building or fish and broccoli invaded her breathing space, Joan wished for the old days. Today, overwhelmed by work, she had forgotten to each lunch, and the smell was hard to resist.

Maybe I could beg some leftovers, she thought. But I don't know when I'd get time to eat them.

The cleanup crew was clattering pots and dishes out in the kitchen. At the far end of the room, a lone figure in a navy pea jacket and knitted hat was still hunched over a plate.

There was something familiar about the posture. Joan went closer.

"Rebecca!"

Her daughter jumped.

"Mom, you startled me, sneaking up like that."

"Sorry. These shoes can't compete with the kitchen noise." Already I'm apologizing to her, Joan thought. "But what in the world are you doing here? I didn't even know you were in town. The quilt show doesn't open for a week." Stop running on at the mouth, she told herself, and by a miracle, she stopped.

"There are lectures and demonstrations ahead of time." Rebecca wiped her plate clean with a piece of biscuit. "You were busy when I arrived, so I followed my nose. They wouldn't let me go away hungry even after they told me it was for old people. They said they had plenty."

She gulped the biscuit and the last of her coffee.

"I did pay."

Prickly as ever.

Hungry, too? She didn't look all that thin, but it was hard to tell, as covered up as she was. Joan ached to hug her. She hesitated. With her hat and coat on, Rebecca looked ready for instant flight.

"Rebecca, I'm so glad to see you. Just surprised, that's all. A good surprise."

Rebecca stood up, stacked her dishes, and carried them to the pass-through counter.

"Best meal I've had in a week," she told the kitchen workers. "Thanks a lot."

Empty-handed then, she turned around and said. "Aren't you even going to hug me?"

Joan's eyes stung with sudden tears. She put out her arms. Rebecca walked in, and for a long moment they held each other tight.

Rebecca let go first. She pulled off her cap, ran her fingers through her dark curls, and began unbuttoning her jacket.

"Guess I'll take off my coat and stay awhile." Her grin, so much like Andrew's and their father's, broke through at last. "Unless you have something better to do."

"Heavens," said Joan. "I forgot what I came in here for. Those women are out there waiting to work on the quilt."

"Quilt? What kind of quilt?" Rebecca sounded interested.

"I don't know. I haven't even looked at it yet. All I know is that the orchestra guild made it for the show, to auction or raffle or something. It still needs some finishing, and I don't know what came over me—I said I'd help."

"I'll believe that when I see it."

"Me too."

They laughed together.

"Would you check the tables?" Joan asked. "Make sure they're clean enough? That's what I came in to do. I'll be right back."

The group had swelled in her absence. Responding to the letter posted on the bulletin board, two of the center's old regulars had arrived. Even Annie Jordan, no more a quilter than Joan, was there with her ever-present knitting.

"I can sew a hem if it comes to that," she said. "But I mostly came for moral support."

Joan apologized for making them wait and took them in to meet her daughter. Rebecca, who was wiping a table with a dry dishtowel, tolerated the inevitable exclamations with considerably better grace than she had shown as a child.

"SO," SAID MABEL DUNN, no longer the mouse of the board meeting, "let's push a couple of tables together and take a look at this masterpiece." Willing hands unwrapped the covering sheet and spread the quilt out.

Joan hadn't known what to expect. What she saw was big enough for a double bed. A latticework of deep reds and purples framed rectangles of royal blue on which the instruments of the orchestra stood out in bas-relief. The trumpet, French horn, trombone, tuba, flute, and harp were gold; the violin, viola, cello, and bass were shades of red and brown; the clarinet, oboe, and English horn gleamed a satiny black. Most of the details were embroidered, but even Joan could see that the tiny white and black keys of the grand piano had been pieced together from separate bits of fabric, as had the light heads and gleaming kettles of the timpani. Near the center the conductor's baton lay below an open score, its notes mere suggestions.

Infinitesimal stitches through all three layers—the decorated top, the puffy batting, and the plain muslin back— drew lines in shadows, the essence of quilting.

"Ohhhhh?" said Annie, drawing the word out in southern Indiana's rising inflection of marveling admiration. "Will you look at that?"

I'll never in this world be able to make such little stitches, Joan thought. And if I could, I wouldn't have the patience.

Rebecca ran her hand over the quilt.

"The intense colors are great, and the textures," she said. "Wool and velveteen, and that shiny gold. And look at the trapunto."

"The what?" Annie asked.

"You know, the stuffing in the instruments. They stuck extra batting in through the back to make them stand out like that."

"It's Dacron," said Mabel, checking the open edge. "Won't fall apart. That's why they could get away with so little quilting. So much the better. Less work for us."

"True," said Carolyn Ryrie. "But I like cotton better. Synthetics just don't have the same feel."

I'll bet you only eat brown rice, too, Joan thought.

"Question is, would you want it on a bed?" Mabel said. "Or do you think it will go for more if we fix it for a wall hanging?"

"Do you have to choose?" Joan wondered whether anyone would buy it at all. What would I do with it if I won? Sleep under kettledrums? Hang it in the living room?

"Not yet," Mabel answered her spoken question. "First we need to carry the quilting to the very edge. It won't take long, even without a frame. It's all but done, and these plain diagonals are easy. Then I'll attach the binding with the sewing machine, and we'll blind-stitch it on the back."

They spread out around the double table, making space for Rebecca, who sat down with them as if she knew what she was doing.

"I don't want to hurt your feelings, Joan," Mabel said. "But you did say you'd never quilted. Would you be willing to keep the needles threaded for the rest of us?"

"Right, Mom," Rebecca said. "That's the job they used to give the children."

Joan wasn't sure she was up to even that. But Mabel showed her how to knot a short length of the strong white thread at one end and run it across a block of beeswax.

"That keeps it from tangling," she explained. "And keep the threads short—less than a foot long. We'll lose more time quilting with a long thread than you can ever save on threading."

Snipping the thread with stork-shaped scissors she had seen last in Edna's hands, Joan clumsily prepared the needles. The beeswax-stiffened thread didn't flop when she missed an eye and bumped an edge. Still, with six quilters, she had to work to keep up.

Fascinated, she watched Rebecca's right hand rock from thimble to point and her left forefinger move rhythmically back and forth, guiding the needle from beneath, until, as if gasping for breath, the needle released half a dozen tiny stitches to the waxed thread and rose in the air before plunging in for more. With no frame to hold it taut, Rebecca stretched her section of quilt between her left hand and the edge of the table, where she anchored it with her right elbow.

Where had she learned this?

"You're hiding your knots, aren't you?" Kitty asked the room in general. "Edna was a real stickler about not letting a knot show. She always said that was the first thing a judge would take off for."

As she spoke, Kitty teased the fabric apart with her needle to start a new thread. A quick, short jerk sent the knot through the top and set it in the batting. Her fingernail nudged the opening closed again, and her right hand began rocking and lifting in the quilter's dance. Kitty's line grew faster than the others, but with a certain flatness.

Looking closely, Joan saw that these stitches were three times as long as Rebecca's. The eye saw a line, not of shadows, but of thread.

"This is nice," said one of the old regulars, stroking a section near the edge. "But it don't hold a candle to Edny's best quilting. Twelve stitches to the inch, and the back always pretty as the top. Or some of them real old quilts she had. You ever see those? Quilted so close you couldn't put your little finger between the lines. If she'd ever showed 'em, she'd've walked off with all kinds of prizes."

"I don't know about that," said another. "Last year's big winner had no more quilting to it than this. It was like one of those wild modern paintings—all colors and no sense. The woman didn't even quilt her own tops. She farmed them out."

"And called herself a quilter?"

"You run into that a lot now." Carolyn Ryrie spoke up.

"You always did," Mabel said. "Our church used to quilt tops for other people. I remember back when we charged five dollars a spool—and used maybe two dozen spools a top. Nowadays it would probably run you a good twenty-five a spool, if you could even find anyone to do it. But no one would quilt that close."

"I was thinking more of the modern paintings," Carolyn said. "Some of my artist friends think I'm silly to want to finish what I design. Too slow, they say. Some don't even piece the top themselves. But I want to control the whole process, from dying the cotton with natural dyes to making my own binding."

"So do I!" Across the table, Rebecca's face lit up. "What kind of natural dyestuffs do you find around here?"

"Come out to my cabin, and I'll show you." Carolyn parked her needle in the quilt. Rummaging in a pocket of her skirt, she came up with a folded sheet of paper. "Here—it's tricky to find without a map."

"What's this?" Mabel, too, held up a piece of paper. It looked to have been torn from a small spiral notebook. "I found it stuck in between the top and the batting. 'No sugar on cereal'?"

Kitty reached for it.

"I'm sorry," she said. "It's one of my notes. I guess Edna slipped it in when I wasn't looking."

No sugar—that would be Edna's diabetes, Joan thought. But why a note about it? And why in the quilt?

The table was silent. For a moment, the hands stopped rocking and lifting. Crumpling the note, Kitty answered the question no one asked.

"She'd been having trouble remembering for some time. It got worse when she was sick. At first she could joke about it, but it really bothered her. So she started writing notes to herself. You know, a note on the front door to remind her to take her keys. That kind of thing."

Kitty passed her empty needle to Joan.

"I do that myself," Joan said, sending back a threaded one.

"But she started needing notes to find things in the kitchen, or to remember to wear a coat," Kitty said. "And then I had to write them—not that she was going out anymore." She jerked her knot all the way through the quilt top and had to start again.

"Sometimes, at the end, she'd hide notes she didn't like. This one was to help her follow her diet." Setting the knot at last, Kitty pulled two long stitches through the layers.

"I've been finding them everywhere—in books, under her nightgowns, stuck on the backs of pictures. Now here.'' She raised her head from her work and looked around the table.

"Don't tell. You knew Edna. She'd just hate it if people knew. Please don't tell.''

SIX

Rolling Stone

"DON'T TELL WHAT, little Kitty?"

Sitting with her back to the door, Joan would have recognized Leon Ellett's voice anywhere.

"Why, Mr. Ellett," she said, and turned from Kitty's stricken face to pull out a chair for him. "Did you come to help? With another worker, we'll be done in no time."

Her own voice rang as false as her words, but he didn't seem to notice. Ignoring the chair, he towered over her, the eyes below his bushy brows fixed on hers.

"Call me Leon," he boomed. "I came to take Kitty back to the house. I thought you'd be done by now."

Mabel Dunn offered, "I can give you a ride, Kitty. Unless you'd rather leave now, of course."

"Thank you, Mabel," Kitty almost whispered. "I want to finish." Her needle rose and dipped as if Leon weren't there.

"We're just getting a good start," Joan told him. "Sure you can't stay?"

"Wouldn't do you any good if I did," he said, smiling down at her.

"That's how I feel." Joan smiled back. Then she realized what she'd said. "About myself, I mean. But they gave me a job where I couldn't do much damage."

"Could they spare you for a minute?"

"Heavens yes," said Mabel. "You go on."

Conscious of Rebecca's eyes, Joan led him out of the room. Does he want to talk about his mother? she wondered. In any case, she'd pulled Kitty's chestnuts out of the fire.

"We could go into my office," she offered.

"Or my car. It's a beautiful day for a drive."

She raised a mental eyebrow. Not his mother, then.

"I can't leave," she said. "But I'll walk you to it." She ducked under the arm holding the outside door for her and crunched across the gravel, inhaling spring air.

"What's on your mind?"

"You," he said. He stopped dead in the middle of the parking lot. "I've been thinking about you ever since I met you at the funeral home."

Good Lord.

He took both her hands in his big paws before she could object. Then she wasn't sure she wanted to. There was something appealing about Leon, oversize personality and all.

"Will you go to dinner with me?"

"Oh, thank you, but I couldn't." It was automatic.

"Why not?" He still held her hands; she didn't pull them away. "I'm single, clean, and you even knew my mother."

Right. Why not? It's only dinner. I'm too old for this game, she mourned. I've forgotten how. And what would Rebecca say?

That settled it.

"Thank you, Leon, I'd love to."

"About seven? I'll come for you."

"Oh, not tonight. I really can't. My daughter just arrived—she's in with the quilters. I haven't seen her for so long. We've barely said hello."

"Tomorrow, then."

"Well . . ."

He sealed it with a bear hug and released her. Then, suddenly businesslike, he held an expectant pen over a little black book that made her want to giggle. She recited her address and phone number with a straight face.

"I'll pick you up at seven," he said, beaming. "Best bib and tucker."

The giggle rose in her throat. Speechless, she waved feebly and ducked back into the building. Through the big front window she watched a red sports car raise a cloud of limestone dust and accelerate into traffic scant feet ahead of a tank truck.

What am I getting into? she thought.

Returning to the group, she found Carolyn Ryrie holding forth on the insensitivity of the local police, and Rebecca, in town not more than an hour, in the amen corner.

"The sergeant called it *laundry!*" Carolyn said. "I'll bet he sits on handmade quilts at picnics—he looks as if he goes to a lot of picnics. He wasn't going to do a thing."

"They're all like that," said Rebecca.

"Well, not all," Carolyn conceded. "The lieutenant promised to circulate a description. And when I valued it at three thousand dollars, he called it felony theft."

"Lieutenant?"

"Older man, but a real hunk."

Joan perked up her ears. Fred?

"Actually, that's why I'm here today," Carolyn said. "I'm glad to help you, but I hope you'll help me, too."

"Of course, if we can," Mabel said.

Carolyn parked her needle again. Pulling a scrap of fabric from her pocket this time, she smoothed it out for the others to see. It was soft cotton, a warm brown with enough variation that Joan was sure Carolyn had dyed it herself. She wondered about some black marks near one edge.

Annie Jordan leaned forward, peered at it, and muttered, "Baby-bottom brown" in Joan's ear.

"Lovely," said Rebecca.

"Is your stolen quilt all this color?" asked Mabel. "And what kind of quilt was it? Pieced? Appliqué? A traditional pattern?"

"No, it's original. The whole quilt is in shades of brown," Carolyn said. "Very simple piecing, all rectangles of different sizes."

"What did you use?" asked Rebecca.

"Hickory hulls for this color," Carolyn said. "Tea. The darkest brown is from black walnut hulls. I alternated plain blocks with my own wood-block prints and printed my designs in black silk-screen ink. You can see just a little of that in the corner of this scrap."

"Did you sign it?"

"No, but there can't be two quilts like this one. The prints are my signature."

"You have slides, of course," Rebecca said.

"No, dammit. It's only the best work I've ever done, but there wasn't time. I finished it the day before the application deadline. That was okay—I live here, and the jury was willing to look at a finished quilt instead of a slide. When it made the show, I took it home and hung it out in the sun to photograph. It disappeared off the line before the light was right."

"What a shame," Joan said.

"Isn't that always the way?" said one of the old regulars.

"What do the prints look like?" asked Mabel.

"They're woodblocks, kind of rough. The designs are abstract, so they're hard to describe. Maybe you've seen molas—I used some of those shapes."

"Never heard of 'em."

"What a great idea! Molas are fantastic!" Rebecca's face glowed. "The San Blas Indian women of Panama make them for their blouses. They're reverse appliqué— layers under layers—all curves and colors." Her left hand escaped from under the quilt to help her talk. "You find them in museum shops sometimes—even the practice molas the little girls make, no bigger than this." Joining its mate, her thimbled right hand framed a postcard in the air. "But the best ones are usually old and worn, with faded colors. A lot of them are abstract. Carolyn, I wish I could have seen your designs."

"I still have the layout," Carolyn said. "And the woodblocks—I printed them on paper for the police. Don't know why I didn't think to bring some today."

"You know," said Joan slowly, "if you could print some on your dyed fabric, I'm sure the committee would be willing to post it at the show with a notice about your stolen quilt. Mary Sue Ellett would be the person to ask."

"She sent me here."

"That's right, you said that. I'll tell her you worked today. This orchestra quilt is her baby."

"Good idea, Mom," said Rebecca, rocking and lifting again. "People come to this show from all over. No matter where the thief takes it, someone might spot it."

"Trouble is, I don't have any more fabric," Carolyn said. She folded her scrap and tucked it back into her pocket. "Once I finished piecing and started quilting, I made the rest into a shirt for a friend of mine."

"Would he lend it to you? Or wear it to the show? Kind of a living poster?" Joan asked. She slipped another waxed thread through its elusive target and twirled the knot as if she'd been doing it for years.

"Um ... I don't think so. That was months ago." Carolyn picked up her needle and started quilting again, avoiding Joan's eyes. "We're not exactly on good terms anymore."

Joan backed off. "Not exactly good" had to be mild for a relationship that could deter this woman from recovering the best work she'd ever done.

For a little while the needles danced on in silence. Then, gradually, each quilter's running stitches met the work of the woman to her left. First to finish her section of the border, Kitty stood up and stretched. Carolyn quickly followed her example.

"Point me to the facilities," she said, and they left the room together. The others wasted no time.

"Who is she, anyway?" asked a regular whose name escaped Joan.

"Never saw her before," said Annie. "Not from around here, that's for sure."

"Her name is Carolyn Ryrie," Joan said. "Mary Sue sent her to help. You know why—she told you about her quilt."

"No, not her. The other one."

"She's that cousin stayed with Edny," said the other quilter whose face was more familiar than her name. "What's her name—Kate?"

"Kitty," Joan said. "Kitty Graf."

"That's it. I told Edny. She's got her eye on the main chance, I said. And I was right. You can't tell me Edny Ellett needed a note to go out the door!"

"Hold your horses, Ruby," said Mabel. "What do those notes have to do with anything?"

Ruby, that's who she was.

"No fool like an old fool," Ruby said shortly, her needle rocking faster with the force of her emotion. "The vultures don't wait till you're dead. And if you look like you've already lost your marbles, it makes it that much easier for them."

"I know all about vultures." Annie brought her knitting to the seat Kitty had vacated. "A real estate man brings me a poinsettia every Christmas. Keeps after me to sell him my house." She chuckled. "Ten years ago I made sure he'd never get it—I wish I could be there to see his face when he hears what's in my will. But this is different, Ruby. Kitty took good care of Edna. And she's not the queerest bird in that family by a long shot. Look at Leon."

Here we go, Joan thought.

"You know he's living on the qt with the oldest Wheatcraft girl," said Mabel, weaving her last stitch back through the batting before bringing it to the surface and snipping the thread.

"Not anymore, he's not." Annie's four knitting needles clicked around the toe of her sock. "She threw him out last fall. I don't know who his meal ticket is now."

"Doesn't matter, does it?" said Mabel. "He looks to come in for a pretty penny from Edna, even split three ways."

Joan was glad to see Kitty and Carolyn return. The last to finish, Rebecca had been working silently.

"Sorry to be so slow," she said as she cut her thread. "I'm new at this."

"That's all right, honey," said Mabel. "Good quilting takes time. But I'll have the binding ready for you in just a little bit." She gathered up the quilt and carried it over to the sewing machine that stood ready in a corner of the activity room.

While Mabel machine-stitched a dark brown binding to the raw edges, Ruby and the other woman put on their coats. Joan thanked them for coming to help.

A few minutes later, she wasn't surprised when Rebecca and Carolyn decided to leave together.

"Carolyn knows how to find your house," Rebecca said. "How soon will you be there to let me in?"

"Andrew might be home now, but it doesn't matter," Joan said. "I made you an extra key so you could come and go on your own."

They collected it from her shoulder bag, hanging on its hook in the office.

"Thanks," Rebecca said. "See you, Mom."

"For supper?"

"I don't know. Don't count on me."

Well, no. Too bad we didn't have this conversation before I turned down a date for tonight. But it's not as if you asked me to. I did that all by myself.

Mabel spread the quilt facedown on the tables to hem the binding. In the sun now slanting through the single window onto the muslin backing, the instruments of the orchestra stood out in outline, even without their colors. All those little stitches, Joan thought. If I hadn't watched them doing it...

Mabel and Annie each took a side, and Kitty took one end, leaving the other to Joan.

Blind-stitching sounded ominous.

"I'd better just watch for a minute," Joan said.

She was reassured to see nothing more complicated than hemming a skirt. Kitty, of the long quilting stitches, was in the running here. Joan set herself to try.

The puffy batting sticking out of the quilt's edges filled the folded binding and made it easy to hide her stitches. But looking down the long row ahead of her, Joan suddenly understood the emperor who had once waved a dismissing hand and said, "Too many notes, Herr Mozart."

The sun was lower and she was only halfway down her side when the other three finished theirs.

"I'll take it home to do that last little bit," Kitty said. "Mary Sue will tell me where to deliver it."

Joan didn't argue.

SEVEN

Widow's Troubles

THE BACKPACK and duffel bag in the silent kitchen had to be Rebecca's. But she wasn't there. No sign of Andrew, either.

Joan put yesterday's ham and beans on the stove. She greased the big cast-iron skillet and put it in the oven to heat up while she mixed a batch of cornbread to bake in it. Swiss chard for greens, she thought—all Rebecca's favorites. Her own, for that matter.

With supper in the works, she sat down to check the paper—obituaries first, but nobody else from the center had died. Then she turned to the funnies. The phone waited just long enough for her to kick off her shoes and put her feet up. She padded back, the kitchen floor cold against her soles.

Alex Campbell sounded as if she might have been climbing stairs—or conducting Wagner.

"Thank God you're home."

"What's the problem, Alex?" Stretching the cord, Joan backed up to the oven's warmth.

"We're going to have to set up for Wednesday, after all. Mary Sue called me this morning. And you know the school janitor wouldn't touch the inn."

Joan knew the janitor. She counted it a minor miracle every time he showed up at a rehearsal. Soothing the players and telephoning the principal to unlock the door when he didn't were among the orchestra manager's less enviable chores.

"Are there at least chairs?"

"Not even that, Joan, what will we do?" Now, away from the podium, Alex was deferring to her.

"Don't worry about it, Alex. I'll think of something." She was already thinking of the complaints she'd hear. Folding chairs from Snarr's, the only practical answer on such short notice, would jab the players in all the wrong places.

Might as well get it over with. With Alex's gratitude still breathless in her ears, she called Bud Snarr at home and promoted not only chairs, but hauling and a man to set them up.

"Long as you show him where," Bud said. "When do you need 'em?"

"We practice Wednesday night. I could come over that afternoon, or Tuesday evening."

"Tuesday's good," Bud said. "Around four?"

Joan kept forgetting how early "evening" started in southern Indiana.

"Is a little past five okay? I get off work at five." And the Sagamore Inn closed at five. Oh, well. She could arrange for a key.

"Sure thing," said Bud.

Joan dialed Mary Sue's number. No answer.

She stewed.

It's bad enough that she's dumping on me again. But she could have called me at work—I was working on her big project, no less. She probably knew what I'd say. So she got Alex involved in something a conductor shouldn't have to worry about. And because it was Alex, I not only said yes, but now I have to find Mary Sue to let me into the building after hours.

Then the simple answer came. Fred Lundquist answered on the second ring.

"Sure, I can let you in," he said. "If you even need letting in. Sounds as if people will be working late tomorrow to hang the show. If they aren't, just come across the street. I'll be there."

Joan chopped the chard with fierce strokes. When Andrew and Rebecca walked in together, she was just pulling the skillet of cornbread out of the oven.

"Timed that right." Andrew shucked his coat. "Think I'll stay."

Rebecca, still in her pea jacket, looked at the kitchen table set for three.

"You were that sure I'd come?" she asked. Back to prickly.

"Nope." Joan reached for a knife. "But I didn't want to hop up in the middle of supper if you turned up at the last minute." She grinned at her daughter. "I'm glad you did."

She cut the cornbread in wedges and set the hot skillet on a tile beside the beans and her last jar of dark woods honey. The farmer's market wouldn't open again until May.

Andrew pulled up a chair and helped himself.

"Bec, you rate the fatted calf. I haven't seen that honey for weeks."

Rebecca didn't answer.

Joan sat down. She slowly crumbled a wedge of cornbread onto her plate and ladled beans over it.

Rebecca finally tossed her coat on her duffel bag, washed her hands at the kitchen sink, and joined them. She went on the attack almost immediately.

"Andrew told me about the orchestra murders last fall. Sounds as if you solved them and gave the police all the credit."

"I helped," Joan said. "I never thought of it that way."

"You'd better start thinking that way, or men will walk all over you. Pass the butter, will you, Andrew?"

"You really believe that?"

"I know it." Rebecca reached for the honey. "My boss makes my ideas sound like his own at first. If they fall flat, he lets everyone know where they came from. You can guess who gets the raise if they pan out."

Joan ached at the bitterness she was hearing. She risked a direct question.

"Are you still at that bank?"

"Two years now. But as soon as I can swing it, I'm going into business for myself."

"Doing what?" Andrew asked.

"I'm designing a specialty line." Rebecca's eyes suddenly danced. "You'll see."

But that's all she would say. Even Andrew couldn't budge her. She changed the subject.

"Mom, tell me about that man Kitty wouldn't go home with. What did he want with you?"

The quilters had given Rebecca a real earful. Joan took a deep breath.

"He asked me out."

"You aren't going!"

How could a daughter make her feel ten years old? Joan laid down her fork and worked to lower her voice.

"Yes, I am. I'm having dinner with Leon tomorrow."

"Mother, he's such a sleaze! The way he looked at you! And didn't you hear what those old ladies were saying about him? He sounds like a real con man. At the bank, widows who've been fleeced by guys like him cry on our shoulders."

Andrew tried to help.

"Great supper, Mom."

Joan waved him off and looked Rebecca in the eye. "Is it really so hard for you to imagine that a man might want to invite me out with no ulterior motives? I've been alone for years. Now I'll see men if I choose. And I'll choose the men I see. Is that clear?"

"I just don't want to see you get taken in by a—"

"Stop right there, Rebecca. You're not the only person with the right to make her own mistakes."

They ate in silence. Rebecca picked at her food.

What got into me? Joan thought. I never talk like that. And what if she's right? I heard what they were saying about Leon. Suppose I'd heard it first—would I have said yes to him?

Loneliness washed over her. Here I am with the two people I love most in the world, she thought, and I feel more alone than when I'm by myself.

It must have shown.

"Hey, Mom, it's okay," said Andrew. "You have a good time. If that Leon bozo steps out of line, I'll sic Lundquist on him."

That broke the tension. Joan laughed, and Rebecca looked confused.

"Who?" she said.

"Mom's cop. You know, the one who got all the credit. He's not so bad." Emptying the skillet, Andrew slathered butter on the last of the cornbread.

"I like him, Rebecca," Joan said. "Maybe while you're here, we could invite him over." Rebecca's going to think I have all kinds of social life I don't.

"If you want to. I'll be in and out." It wasn't exactly gracious, but it was a start.

Joan leaned forward. "Tell me about Carolyn Ryrie. You and she seemed to hit it off."

Rebecca brightened. "We just got started, but I'm going to visit her—maybe on the weekend."

"Is there any chance you and Andrew would go to church with me on Sunday?" The words were out before Joan knew she was going to say them.

"Church?" Andrew said. "Mom, you haven't gone to church once since we came to Oliver. Why now?"

"It might do her good after Leon," said Rebecca. "Honestly, Andrew, wait till you meet this guy. But I don't know about going. Maybe."

Why now, indeed? Joan knew enough not to expect the preacher to be another Ken. Or the congregation to cut through her loneliness. Back home—after months in Oliver she still thought of Michigan as home—she had found comfort, if not inspiration, in her somewhat sporadic attendance after Ken's death. His old congregation had felt like her extended family. But in Oliver she hadn't forced herself to walk into a church where no one would even know who she was.

"I guess I feel more like a family with both of you here," she said. "And it might not be so bad. We never sat with Dad in church."

Tears glinted in Rebecca's eyes. "Only on vacations," she said. "He used to play hangman with me."

WHEN THE RED sports car pulled up on Saturday, Andrew was posted at the front door.

Upstairs, Joan was in an uncharacteristic dither about what to wear. This is silly, she thought. I'm not even interested in the man.

Peeking out the window, she saw that Leon Ellett's "best bib and tucker" was a crimson sports coat, not a dinner jacket. Good. Her long-sleeved blue wool would be fine. She finished buttoning it to the throat.

She smoothed back the wisps of front hair that were already escaping from the French roll she'd shaped for the occasion. Then she slipped on her pumps, picked up her bag, and went down to him.

Sitting in her biggest chair with his back to her, Leon was already deep in conversation with Rebecca. Joan wondered how he had managed that. Rebecca enlightened her.

"Hi, Mom. Mr. Ellett is telling me all about banking. It's really fascinating." Rebecca batted her eyelashes at him. "Did you know that you could make a killing in real estate just by taking advantage of the time it takes banks to process their checks?"

Leon jumped to his feet as Joan descended the stairs. He answered Rebecca with a chuckle.

"I wouldn't say that, little lady. But I've turned some nice little profits in my day. It's all in understanding how the system works."

Rebecca radiated wide-eyed innocence. Leon turned his smile on Joan.

"I hope you don't mind my talking to your daughter. You could have knocked me over with a feather when I saw her—I would have sworn you couldn't have a grown child."

"Two of them," Joan said dryly. "You've met Rebecca. And this is my son. Andrew, Mr. Leon Ellett."

Leon pumped Andrew's hand.

"Don't worry about your lovely mother, son. I'll bring her home safe and sound."

"Yes, sir," said Andrew, pumping back. "Thank you, sir. We do worry if she's out too late."

Rebecca rolled her eyes, but Andrew's face was almost wooden. For the second time in Leon's presence, Joan had to stifle the urge to giggle. He was hard enough to take seriously without those two.

Andrew opened the door for them.

The cold of a spring evening hit her face, and a brisk wind attacked her hair. At the curb, Leon gripped her elbow—a useless and uncomfortable gesture, Joan thought, and one that made her feel at least thirty years older. Then he handed her into the little red two-seater, and they roared off.

By the end of an excellent steak dinner at the Elks Club, Joan was sorry she had come. Leon flirted with the waitress, ate, and talked nonstop—about Leon. Flashing an outsize diamond pinky ring, he went from his big real estate developments to his cash-flow problems.

Must be a zircon, Joan thought.

He led her onto the dance floor, where his guiding arm was as strong as his steps were graceful. But the subject didn't change.

"My mother's estate will make the difference," he said at last. "But time means nothing to lawyers. It could take months. Meanwhile, I'm sitting on an option to some choice property that will...well, never mind. I don't want to bore you."

Joan knew she was supposed to say, "You're not boring me at all," but truthfulness and optimism stopped her from encouraging him.

"I'm glad I knew your mother," she said instead. "I'm only sorry I came along too late to know her better." Or in her prime, she thought.

As if he'd heard her, Leon said, "You remind me of her when she was young and pretty. She was gentle with us— but strong enough to make me toe the line. Little as she was, she didn't put up with any nonsense."

"Did you test her?"

He grinned down at her, and she saw the teddy bear again.

"Every way a boy could. Once—I was about eight—she had us all spiffed up for a company dinner, with orders to entertain the company's children while the grown-ups visited. So I took their two little boys down to play king of the mountain in the coal bin."

Joan laughed out loud—and missed a step.

"What happened?"

"We came when she called us for dinner. She took one look, marched us upstairs, stripped us, and had us in a hot tub before we could blink. Then she laid out some of my outgrown clothes for them and told me that if I wanted any dinner, I'd better scrub those boys as clean as I'd gotten them dirty."

He grinned again. "The food was stone cold by the time we came down to eat. But it was worth it."

The music stopped, Leon twirled her, and they went back to their table for coffee. When the check came, he paid with plastic and signed with a flourish.

Outside, the cold had strengthened. Joan shivered and welcomed his warm arm around her shoulders. At her door, though, she was relieved that he didn't invite himself in. But why would he? she thought. He's already met my chaperones.

"I'd like to see you again," he said.

She stuck out her right hand and smiled. "Thank you, Leon," she said. "It was a lovely dinner."

Holding her hand, he stooped and kissed her gently on the cheek.

"Good night, little Joan," he said, and brushed wisps of hair back off her face. "See you in church."

You just might, she thought. I wonder which of us would be more surprised.

From the doorway she watched Leon slide down into the little car. He revved up the engine and beeped "Shave and a haircut, two bits."

He's a big kid, she thought. The world is his oyster, even if he's going broke. I wonder what it would take to get him down.

She found Rebecca and Andrew stretched out on the living room floor, talking.

"Have a good time?" asked Andrew.

"Sure," Joan said.

"Well?" asked Rebecca. But Joan had no desire to dissect Leon with Rebecca. Nor with anyone else she could think of.

"Good night, you two," she said, and went upstairs.

Their voices murmured her to sleep.

EIGHT

Basket of Lilies

JOAN WOKE TO Bartók. Was "Saint Paul Sunday Morning" featuring Hungarians? She rolled over, luxuriating in weekend freedom. Then she smelled the coffee. And popovers. Popovers?

"You ready for church, Mom?" Andrew called up the stairs.

"Are you kidding?" Her tongue was still thick with sleep.

"We've decided to go. If you want to come, you have ten minutes for a shower before breakfast."

Would wonders never cease? Her feet hit the floor.

She twisted her hair out of harm's way, turned the shower on hot, and felt tepid needles sting her skin. Bad enough to follow Andrew—this morning she was probably third in line. Hurrying, she got out before the old hot-water tank went completely cold.

The open window dispelled the bathroom fog and gave her goose bumps. Still cool enough for the blue wool. She dried off, put her clothes on, and went downstairs.

"Take a seat, Mom," Andrew said from the stove. Joan obeyed, accepting the juice and coffee Rebecca poured out, and then Andrew's popovers. The woods-honey jar was on the table.

Too bad Fred's not here, she thought, remembering the September day he had taken popovers out of her oven. But memories of grim death crowded in—he'd been called away to investigate the murder of the orchestra's first flutist, and with the taste of the popovers still in her mouth, she, too, had landed in the flutist's once-cozy kitchen. She shivered.

Maybe that's why I haven't made them since.

"Mom?" said Rebecca. "You okay?"

"I'm fine," she said, and bit into a beautifully browned popover, savoring its egginess and enjoying the crisp outside and slippery inside. "Mmmm. Andrew. what is it about you and eggs?"

"Good, aren't they? You never told me these things were so simple. I finally got hungry enough for them to read the book."

They walked to church.

Sitting in a strange pew between Andrew and Rebecca, Joan returned the smiles on a few familiar faces. It figured—gray hair predominated here, and most of the people she knew best were over sixty. *No one pushed me to come, though,* she thought gratefully. *Did you know they were being kind? Or am I wrong? Would it have been kinder if they had pushed?*

After the Bach prelude announced in the order of worship, the organist meandered on until a balding man in his thirties entered the chancel and sat down. Then she struck up "Cwm Rhondda." The stirring Welsh hymn tune raised the hairs on the back of Joan's neck.

"Grant us wisdom, grant us courage, for the facing of this hour," she sang from memory. Andrew, ignoring the staid harmony printed in the hymnbook, echoed "of this hour" in the old tradition. He grinned at her. A couple of stanzas later, she exchanged smiles with her daughter when Rebecca's alto rang out on "rich in things and poor in soul."

Worth coming for.

The sermon text was the story of the prodigal son, but the young minister began with Thornton Wilder's *Our Town*, and Emily's discovery on returning from the grave to relive her sixteenth birthday.

"It's true, you know," he said. "Emily and the prodigal both learned it the hard way. When things are going well, we don't notice what is most precious to us. The sameness of everyday routine blinds us. Our lives fly by faster with every passing year.

"But death tore young Emily from the family she didn't know how to cherish. The prodigal son treasured the love that had surrounded him only after he had rejected it—and was separated from it by his own foolish decisions. We, too, often recognize our true riches only when we have been separated from them in prisons of our own making, as he was—or by walls of pain, loneliness, fear, or despair.

"Then, as Emily did—as Goethe's Faust did—we cry out at last to the moment: Stay, you are so beautiful."

Joan's mind wandered to the walls she felt around her. Loneliness, yes. Fear?

And she thought of others. What must the prison of Edna Ellett's last weeks have been like, for her, and for Kitty? And what kept Rebecca at such a distance? Who had put those walls up? Were they weakening?

The minister had moved to the power of messages from prisons. He dwelled for a time on Saint Paul. Then he returned to the twentieth century and a name Joan knew well.

"Dietrich Bonhoeffer may have put it best even before he was imprisoned. While heading an illegal seminary in Nazi Germany, he wrote: 'It is true, of course, that what is an unspeakable gift of God for the lonely individual is easily disregarded and trodden underfoot by those who

have the gift every day.' In his own isolation, Bonhoeffer
saw the gift of community as extraordinary, as grace. He
called it the 'roses and lilies' of the Christian life.''

Yes, Joan thought. Lost again in her own thoughts, she
missed the rest of his words.

They sang "Blessed Be the Tie That Binds" and went
out.

Quickly, the buzz of community overwhelmed the post-
lude.

"Let's check out the coffee hour," said Andrew. As a
child, he'd always been first to raid the cookies baked to
welcome visitors. Since then his capacity had expanded.
An hour after eating a dozen popovers, he was ready to
dive in again.

"Okay," said Rebecca. "Do you mind, Mom?"

Mind? Joan was inhaling roses and lilies. Now Margaret Duffy was coming over. Farther down the hall, she
saw Alvin Hannauer swimming upstream to greet them.

"I'd love to. But will you stand still for a couple of introductions? Here come my old teacher and a man who
worked with your grandfather before you were born.
They've both been good to me."

They didn't need to stand still. The crowd swept them all
into a room where the noise was subdued by carpeting.
Andrew spotted the refreshment table in seconds. So did
Alvin. He herded them over to coffee, lemonade, and an
astonishing variety of beautiful cookies.

"You picked a good day to come," Alvin said. "Catherine's stuff beats all."

"Catherine?" Joan asked.

"Catherine Turner. She owns Catherine's Catering,"
said Margaret. And, turning to the attractive woman behind the coffeepot, "But you do this for love, don't you,

Catherine? Have you met Joan Spencer yet? And Andrew and Rebecca?''

"I don't think so," said Joan. But she'd seen that red hair somewhere recently.

Catherine looked through her.

"I think we're out of coffee," she said. She picked up the pot and marched off to the kitchen.

So much for community, Joan thought. What was *that* about?

Margaret made no excuses for Catherine. Margaret wouldn't. Alvin looked awkward, but Andrew ignored the whole thing and dug into the Mexican wedding-cake cookies.

"Try one of these, Mom," he said. "They're terrific."

"No, thanks," said Joan. "I'm ready to go home. Okay, Rebecca?" She nodded to Alvin, squeezed Margaret's hand, and left.

They threaded their way through knots of churchgoers to the sidewalk. The noon sun beat down on Joan's face and back. She was wilting fast.

"What was eating that woman?" Rebecca demanded once they were free of the crowd.

Andrew finished a last mouthful. "I'll bet she's the one Lundquist bakes for."

Rebecca was blank for only a moment.

"The cop?"

"Yeah. Remember, Mom? That day he was at our house, he'd been baking bread for some friend with a catering service." Then he looked at her face. "Woops. Sorry."

Good thing I don't have to drive, Joan thought. I'd probably hit someone.

NINE

Swarm of Bees

ON TUESDAY Joan walked from work to the police station.

Climbing worn limestone steps to a desk that almost reached her chin, she felt like a child again and half-expected her old librarian to scold her for leaving chocolate thumbprints on a book.

But the young man behind the glass looked more like Andrew. She smiled up at him.

"I'm Joan Spencer," she said into the grille. "Fred Lundquist has a key for me."

He picked up a phone and spoke into it so softly that she couldn't hear what he was saying about her.

"Wait there, please, ma'am," he said, pointing to a wooden bench along the wall.

Joan took a hard seat at one end and looked around. Not much to see. Two men in sports coats chatting at the vending machines down the hall, doors marked MEN and WOMEN, a flight of steps where the hall turned left.

Stale butts threatened to overflow the ashtrays at both ends of the bench. She slid to the middle, but the bench was too short to help her nose.

It was quieter than she'd expected. The words of the men at the vending machines didn't reach her ears. From behind the desk came occasional computer beeps and unintelligible bursts from the police radio, the volume lower than she'd ever heard it.

Maybe that's because they're right on top of it here, she thought. Nothing like when they're outside.

Then Fred came trotting down the stairs, pulling on a jacket and smoothing his remaining blond hair. Older, but a hunk, Carolyn What's-her-name had said, and Joan had been sure she meant Fred.

She went to meet him.

"Fred, I'm awfully glad to see you." (Where have you been all winter?) "But I'm sorry to put you out like this."

"It's no trouble." He took the hand she offered and smiled down at her, crinkling the corners of his blue eyes. "You may not even need the key. They're still hard at it. Come on, I'll walk you over."

He waved a forefinger at the desk as they went by, held the door for her, and strolled across the street with her to the Sagamore Inn. No small talk.

Outside, he inhaled deeply. No wonder, Joan thought, glad to be back in air worth breathing.

Up close, the racket coming from the inn's unscreened windows left no doubt that, at half past five, "they" were indeed hard at something.

"Oh, Fred, you're right," she said ruefully. "It *is* still open. I should have checked for myself."

"I need to look in anyway, check on the kids."

"Kids?"

"A couple of kids spend the night with the quilts. Sometimes more than a couple—it gets to be a revolving slumber party. We're on call if there's trouble."

The heavy door didn't yield when Fred tried the latch. Joan felt better. She couldn't have walked in by herself, after all. He eased a key into the Yale lock, turned, and pulled. The door swung open and the noise poured out.

"They'd never have heard me," Joan said.

"Might not have let you in if they had. They're kind of jumpy this year."

"Mary Sue Ellett knows me." And it's her fault I'm even here.

"Yes." His eyes crinkled again. "I found that out."

Joan didn't ask. Maybe he would have said more, but just then a blue van with "Snarr's Funeral Home" on the side pulled up the curving drive. The sandy-haired man who hopped out wore blue jeans and a checked shirt. Tall and wiry, he looked more like a woodsman than a mortician.

"You the lady from the orchestra?" he asked. And, when she nodded, "Bud says you need chairs."

"See you," Fred said, and went on in. Then he stuck his head back out. "I'll prop the door for you, Joan. It's self-locking. Just pull it shut."

"Okay. Thanks, Fred." She turned to Bud Snarr's helper. "You unload them and bring them in while I find out where to set them up, okay?"

"Sure thing." He pulled the back doors open and vaulted into the rear of the van.

Joan left him to it and went into the front hall. The din made her think kindly of trumpets. Mostly it was hammering, punctuated by occasional bursts of a power saw, with people constantly yelling to make themselves heard.

No sign of Fred. Dodging two young women sprinting past her, both loaded down with quilts, she stared at their attire: blue jeans, T-shirt—and white gloves.

"Who's there?" The shout came from a skirted table piled high with bulging pillowcases and plastic bags through which she could see patchwork. Startled, she jumped.

"Joan Spencer," she called back. "From the orchestra." Where was Mary Sue? She felt silly talking to pillowcases.

Now white-gloved hands pushed them apart and revealed a little dumpling of a woman behind a table stacked with folded quilts. The woman picked up a clipboard and a pencil, flipped pages with the eraser, and ran a finger down one without actually touching it.

"Spencer? I'm not finding you." She scrutinized Joan, who was leaning over the table to hear. "And I'm afraid you'll have to tuck that necklace away, dear, and your watch. We can't have you snagging a quilt. What committee did you say you're on?"

Joan checked her watch—quarter to six—and left it on her wrist.

"No committee. I've come to set up for the symphony rehearsal."

"In the middle of all this?"

"I hope not," Joan said fervently. "We're not rehearsing until tomorrow night. Will it still be this noisy in here?"

"Heavens, no! The judges are already here. We started hanging yesterday."

Judges? Hanging? It sounded grim.

Flipping pages again, the woman ran on.

"It's a subjective business, don't you know. We can't outguess the judges completely. You always want the winners up front, but if we waited for them, we'd never open on time. So we do the best we can. We put the ones we think are likely to win in front, and hope that something huge we've hung in back doesn't mess up all our arrangements by winning best in show. We need to get them all up by this time tomorrow—they'll be judging and giving lectures and demonstrations before the show opens Sunday."

The hanging judges had disappeared as quickly as Joan's imagination had conjured them up.

"There it is!" the woman said with satisfaction. "Oliver Civic Symphony—what did you say your name was?"

Joan told her again. She looked up from her clipboard.

"The manager! Why didn't you say so? You want the ballroom. That's where you'll be playing." A pristine forefinger pointed the way.

"Is Mary Sue Ellett here?"

"She's in and out—I haven't seen her lately."

Joan could understand why.

Blue Jeans ran up to the table, peeling off white gloves and ignoring Joan.

"Polly, isn't the Ellett list done yet? I've got to take it over before six."

Flipping pages again, Polly detached two from her clipboard and handed them over.

"You're a doll—the printer's tearing his hair." The jeans disappeared through the front door.

"They're hanging a special display of Edna Ellett's quilts in a room upstairs," Polly told Joan. "We had to change the program at the last minute. You might try up there."

Mary Sue hadn't lost a week because of her mother's death, after all. She'd gained a special display.

"Thanks." Following the noise, Joan walked into a spacious room. On one side, two men hammering two-by-fours onto wooden whirligig bases were putting together something like tall hat racks, with holes up where the hooks should have been. Between bangs, they were carrying on a lively conversation. The polished wooden floor and walls echoed and magnified each blow.

Had Alex listened to these bathtub acoustics before agreeing to play here? She'd like the big sound, but every miserable mistake would carry.

Too late now. At least the room was beautiful, with graceful stairways curving from each side up to a circular walkway, its banisters dark against the white wall. Standing in the center, Joan stretched her neck back to look at the ceiling two stories above. It made her dizzy.

Through open doors she saw three women bent over a quilt spread out on a table in the next room. Beyond them, a few quilts were already hanging between standards like the ones whose construction had nearly deafened her.

"Let's check the back," she heard clearly, and realized that the hammering had stopped. Three pairs of white gloves turned the quilt over, and the debate began.

"This'll never make it. You can see the knots. Here's one, and there—and there's another."

"But the design is spectacular!"

"Won't save it, not with Duckworth judging. She's a real stickler. I vote we put it halfway back. Maybe next to that blue Barn Raising." The others nodded. They slid a pole into a cloth sleeve sewn to the back of the quilt. Two of them carried the pole to the tall stepladders standing ready beside a pair of those odd-looking standards, while the third kept the quilt from dragging on the floor. Joan watched them insert the pole into one of the holes and then turned back to the ballroom.

More women carrying quilts up the stairs gave her an idea of the traffic pattern.

All right, she thought. If the orchestra sits between the two stairways, people can choose between standing to listen and just walking by on their way from one exhibit to another. It's dark under the balcony. Will the folks sitting there be able to read the music? Maybe, but I'll sure hear about it.

Making a mental note to find stand lights, she headed back to the door and picked up a chair under each arm. Snarr's helper came in with four more.

"Here's the last of the load. Where do you want 'em?"

"We're going to be in here," she told him, and took off for the ballroom. He followed, looking around at the few quilts that were already hanging.

"This is something else," he said. "Wonder what kind of beating they'd take if someone got careless with matches around this old place a couple of days from now."

Joan shuddered.

"Don't even think it!" But she looked at the old plank floors with a new eye.

"I wouldn't worry," he said cheerfully. "They're probably insured to the gills." He unfolded his chairs next to hers and went back for more.

Twenty minutes later, they had finished setting up. She counted seats. Eight in the innermost row—her mind's eye saw the two first violins, two seconds, two cellos, and two violas. Flutes and oboes in the second row, with the strings fanning out on either side of them. Clarinets and bassoons in the third, horns and brass in the back.

"We're in good shape," she told the man. "I'm not going to worry about setting up for the basses and percussion. No matter where we put them, Alex is sure to move them. We have enough chairs—that's the main thing. Thanks so much. And tell Bud I'm grateful."

"Bud said he owed it to Mary Sue Ellett—I guess she's in charge of this whole affair."

"That's right. Do you know her, too?"

"Wish I didn't. She still hasn't paid me for some electrical work I did six months ago. But I didn't take it out on her mother."

Joan processed that.

"You worked for Edna, too?"

"Embalmed her and laid her out." Oh. "I do a lot of the work in Snarr's back room. Bud's getting old, and Gil would rather wear a suit and run funerals."

"Well, thank them anyway."

"Sure thing," he said, and left. She heard the big door slam.

By now the foot traffic had stopped and the group from the next room had adjourned. Beyond it, the entrance hall was dark. Along the ballroom wall the carpenters' tools lay in a grove of new support posts and fresh-cut poles that smelled like Christmas.

In the blessed quiet, Joan thought for a moment that she was alone in the building. Then she heard something crash to the floor upstairs. Must be Fred and the kids. Or Mary Sue? Probably no point in asking for stand lights. But she climbed the stairs anyway.

Light and warmth streamed out of one room. She walked around the curve to the doorway and was stopped by a mammoth Double Wedding Ring quilt hanging just inside. Its flamboyant colors made the Double Wedding Ring her Grandma Zimmerman had pieced out of sugar sacks look anemic, even in her memory.

Intense whispers filtered through the quilt.

"She'd never leave it to you."

"I know what she left me."

"Don't you count on it! She said you could talk the hind leg off a mule. But not even you could talk her into that. I'll stop you. You have no right."

Joan was torn between fascination and wanting to tip-toe away before she was caught listening. Someone else must be in the room—why else would these two be whispering? They couldn't know she was there. But she knew the words she was hearing weren't meant for her.

Feeling melodramatic, she went back to the stairs to make noise.

"Fred?" she called, as she came around the curve again. "Mary Sue? Are you all right?"

This time Mary Sue stuck her head out the door.

"Hello, Joan. Don't worry about the racket. We just knocked over one of Mother's quilts—we're hanging them. Come see them. She'd like that."

That's not the way I heard it, Joan thought. But maybe she would, at that. Family and friends are different from a public exhibit.

They were all there. Mary Sue, Alice, Kitty. Leon and a little man in glasses, with a curly brown fringe around his bald head, whom Mary Sue introduced as Harold, Alice's husband, were hauling ladders around the room and sweating freely. No one looked embarrassed.

Good. They don't know I heard.

A dozen quilts were already spaced between the wall and the antiques that gave the old inn its charm.

"Did Edna make them all?" All those little stitches?

"She made two or three a year until her sight got so bad," said Mary Sue. "Most of these are hers, but some have been handed down in the family."

Alice pointed to a crazy quilt of dark silks and velvets, spread out on a maple trundle bed. "I love to stroke this one. I used to beg to sleep under it. Sometimes she'd let me."

"That should be yours, Alice," Mary Sue said. "Unless, of course, Mother willed it to someone outside the family." She turned to Joan. "We don't know about her will yet. It's a nuisance."

Leon muttered something. Harold laughed. Kitty, stitching a folded strip of cloth across the back of a quilt, didn't say anything.

Joan made sympathetic noises. But she wondered about the words she had overheard. There had never been any secret about the content of the wills her own family's lawyers had taken so long to work through.

She wondered, too, whether Mary Sue was being as generous as she sounded. Was a worn crazy quilt as valuable as, say, the well-preserved one in soft green and rose, with the tiny, dense quilting stitches? She pointed to it.

"Tell me about this one."

"Oh, that's one of those that came down from Rachel Berry," said Alice. "Mother always made over Rachel— her great-great-grandmother. She was thrilled to inherit her things."

"Rachel impressed everyone," Leon said. "She made a point of it." He swapped grins with Joan, his boyish appeal in full force.

"That branch of the Berry's went broke a long time ago," he said. "We just got leavings. But Alice is right. To hear Mom, anything from Rachel was solid gold. Trouble is, I need a little of the real kind."

Joan's stomach growled. She fought back a yawn.

Past time to get out of here. I don't need to listen to Leon tonight.

"Mary Sue, I've got the orchestra set up downstairs for tomorrow night. The lighting is uneven down there—we're going to need some stand lights and extension cords."

"Some what lights?"

"Stand lights. You know. They clip on the music stands."

"Never heard of them."

Oh, well. It was worth a try. "I'll try to borrow some. If we have to rent them for this shindig, I'll send you the bill. You want to come check where I've put us?"

"I'm sure you know what you're doing." Mary Sue was already waving to Leon and Harold to move their ladders over to the fallen quilt.

Joan hadn't really expected her to bother checking, not after passing the buck twice. She started down the stairs—and looked over the railing to admire her handiwork.

A tornado had cut its way through her careful seating pattern. Jumbled every which way, the chairs had been pushed out to the sides. A broad swath of open floor gleamed from the concertmaster's spot back to a small door behind the second trumpet's.

"What's going on here?" Joan ran the rest of the way down as if she weren't ready to drop. There was no mistaking the flaming hair framed in the open door.

"That's what I want to know," said Catherine. On Sunday, Joan hadn't been sure. Tonight, though, Catherine's hostility was plain. "*You* did that?" they asked simultaneously, and glared at each other.

This might be funny in a hundred years.

"Yes, I did." Joan struggled to keep her voice from going shrill. "Who gave you the right to tear it up?"

"Who gave you the right to block the kitchen door? I have to set up here for the judges' reception tomorrow!"

Oh. Joan made a stab at peace.

"Sorry." And she almost was. "The left hand must not be talking to the right around here. I set up the orchestra where they told me to, and I just now cleared it with Mary Sue Eilett." She glanced upstairs.

"You sure you have the right Ellett?" Catherine asked sweetly. "I saw you out with Leon the other night. Leon, when you had a chance at Fred. You're a bigger fool than Linda Lundquist.''

Joan gaped, and shut her mouth.

Catherine smiled.

"Better keep your eye on Leon. But then, you won't have any trouble doing that, will you? I hear meddling in other people's affairs is your forte."

She pronounced it "fortay," as in loud.

Joan dug out the seating diagram. Willing her fingers not to shake, she laid it on the closet chair.

"I expect to find it like this tomorrow night at seven," she said.

And left.

TEN

After the Fall

THE NEXT EVENING, Bud's chairs were back in some semblance of order, and the acoustics were greatly improved.

In the midst of the hammering, Joan had despaired that the ballroom's polished wooden floors and walls would be much too "live," jumbling the notes that ricocheted off them. Now the quilts hanging along the walls and from the balcony overheard were making all the difference. The Copland "Hoedown" had a rollicking clarity, and not even the fanfare was too loud.

Enjoying it, Joan looked through the open doors into a room now hung with row upon colorful row, like laundry lines gone wild.

Rebecca had prepared her for quantity, but the variety astonished her. Here, muted tones blended subtly. There, colors rioted. And over there, shadings tricked her eyes into seeing three dimensions where there were only two. Traditional geometric and floral patterns rubbed shoulders with abstractions that might have been painted by Mondrian or Kandinsky.

On the wall nearest her, rosy brown lovers hung intimately entwined in overstuffed embrace. Looking closely, Joan saw that this oddity was really a double sleeping bag. The lovers' soft-sculpture heads would pillow those of the sleepers, who might blush to see a photograph of the resulting effect—if anybody blushed anymore. She nudged John Hocking with her left elbow.

"Look at that one." The fanfare ended in the middle of her sentence. She dropped her voice.

"Wild, isn't it?" he murmured, reaching out to stroke a bare bottom. "Any relation?"

Joan stared. But his face wore only its usual cheerful expression. He leaned back to let her read the neatly printed label basted to one corner.

AFTER THE FALL
REBECCA SPENCER $2000

And she'd been trying to picture Rebecca piecing little squares! She should have known better. Was the price possible?

Maybe she can't bear to part with it, Joan thought. But if she's really pulling in that kind of money, I can quit worrying about her. She said something about designing a line . . .

"You all right?" It was John.

"Oh . . . sorry." She came back. "I'm fine. I didn't exactly expect this." She grinned at him. "Rebecca's my daughter."

"I thought maybe." Now he was laughing.

"I wonder if this is the only thing she entered." She was suddenly wild to know.

"Go ahead. I'll cover for you in the Ives."

"The Ives, oh..." She'd forgotten. "There goes my last chance at it. I promised Alex I'd set up the trumpeter on the balcony." She was already loosening her bow. "You can cover for me Sunday, too."

While Alex rehashed the fanfare with the brasses, Joan tucked her viola into its case, under the old blue velvet blanket. I suppose I could ask Rebecca to quilt me a new one, she thought, feeling the bare threads in the worn spot over the bridge. If I could afford her.

She started up the curving stairway to the balcony.

"Joan!" Alex bellowed.

"Right here."

"Are you ready for the 'Unanswered Question'?"

"Sure. Come on, Eddie."

All joints, ears, and Adam's apple, Eddie bounded up the stairs.

"Do you think he'll sound better on top, or halfway down the stairs?"

"As far away as possible. But where he can see me! I can't do this on Sunday." Alex was craning her short neck.

"Let's try around here," Joan said, and Eddie followed her around the balcony until they were looking directly at Alex from over the trumpet section. The violas and Rebecca's sleeping bag were invisible under the stairs on the left.

Alex nodded, held a finger to her lips, and pointed at the concertmaster, who stood up to beat a steady four for the strings. Almost inaudible chords—whispers—rose to the balcony. Alex pointed to Eddie.

Raising his silver trumpet, he played five haunting notes—Ives's "question." Eddie had a clear, sweet tone even a violist could love. Joan was sorry when Alex broke the spell.

"Too close. Eddie, you should be coming from a mile away. Can't you back up?"

They were already backed against the wall, hung with quilts. Joan knew that the closed doors all around the balcony hid rooms filled with others.

"In there?" Eddie asked, pointing to the nearest door.

"Try it," came from below.

It opened easily, and Eddie disappeared. Softer now, the plaintive trumpet question floated out over the balcony.

"Perfect!" Alex cried.

Eddie came to the door. "I can't hear a thing in there," he complained. "And I can't see you. How will I get my cue?"

"Easy," said Alex, unfazed by details now that she had the sound she wanted. "Joan, you cue him."

"I don't know, Alex," Joan said, dubious.

"Nothing to it," Alex promised. "Come on, try. We don't have all night."

Eddie rolled his eyes and disappeared again into the darkness. Joan heard a crash and a muttered curse.

"Are you all right?" she called into the darkness.

"Not if I bent my trumpet. Where the hell are the lights?"

Reassured, she felt for the switch and flooded the room with light. On the far side Eddie was scrambling to his feet near a limestone fireplace with a Franklin stove extending into the room, the precious trumpet safe in one outstretched hand. But Joan groaned at the devastation around him. And she recognized the brilliant Double Wedding Ring quilt now hanging along one side wall. This was the Ellett room. She sighed.

"Mary Sue Ellett will have a duck fit."

"Huh?" Clearly, Eddie was oblivious to the quilts crumpled on the floor.

"It's all right, Eddie. You couldn't help it. I would've grabbed them, too, if I'd gone down like that."

Seeing them at last, he shook his head.

"I didn't grab anything."

"Don't worry. I'll deal with Mary Sue. Come on. We'd better do the Ives before Alex skins us alive." She picked up the old-fashioned sadiron that must have tripped him and set it on the walnut mantelpiece.

The rest of the piece went well. Joan relayed cues to Eddie as if she'd been conducting all her life. Leaving the strings to the concertmaster, Alex beat a contrasting rhythm for the quartet of flutes, whose last notes tumbled all over each other—no "answer" at all.

Hearing the Ives from between the trumpet and the strings and flutes sent chills down Joan's spine.

And to think the composer spent his life as an insurance salesman.

At last Alex was satisfied and declared a break. From the balcony, Joan made a couple of routine announcements, ending with a reminder.

"We don't play until Sunday. Between now and then there'll be judging and lectures. We'll be held responsible for any mess they find in the morning. So please take a look around your seat before you leave today."

Down below, the chatter started. At her elbow, Eddie said, "I really didn't grab those covers, but I'll help you put 'em back."

"Thanks, Eddie." No point in arguing. She only hoped they weren't damaged. She'd never hear the end of it from Mary Sue as it was.

While Eddie laid his trumpet safely on the mantelpiece, Joan studied the quilts that were still hanging. She had hoped for something simple, like clothespins. But she should have remembered. The Elletts had hung Edna's quilts on poles by the same method she'd seen used downstairs, but in spite of his protests, it was clear that their basting stitches had yielded to Eddie's weight. This was no quick-fix job.

Eddie was right about one thing. He could at least help pick up the fallen quilts before they got any dirtier. But he was just standing there, holding one corner of the nearest one and staring down at the floor.

"Eddie? Are you okay?"

He looked a little green around the gills.

Then she saw it, too.

A slingback pump with a three-inch heel. A foot protruding from a green polyester pant leg. And, when she threw back the quilt, a plastic bag clinging to a square face, the color drained from it.

This isn't happening, Joan thought. It's not real.

She stooped to confirm what she already knew. Touching that foot was like touching a dressed fryer in the supermarket. Chicken under nylon.

"She's cold." Joan felt as sick as Eddie looked. "And stiff."

"That—that was in here the whole time?" he croaked.

Joan nodded. "Go across the street and get the police, Eddie."

Eddie bolted for the stairway.

Joan sat down on the floor. She wouldn't have to call Mary Sue, after all.

THE CHICKEN WAS just beginning to smell like food when the phone in Fred's kitchen rang.

"Sorry to bother you at home, Lieutenant," the dispatcher said. "But a kid ran in here a couple minutes ago pointing at the inn and yelling something about not grabbing quilts. Then he fell apart. I can't get any sense out of him. You want me to send someone across the street?"

"No, I'll come. Keep him there."

Fred turned off the oven and slapped some mozzarella between a couple of slabs of his own bread. He'd long since quit trying to deal with crises on an empty stomach.

Chewing as he drove back to the station, he was glad he'd already changed clothes. Maybe his Mister Rogers sweater would have a calming effect.

He didn't recognize the skinny kid trembling on the bench by the desk, but the dispatcher nodded yes when he tilted his head that way.

"I'm Lieutenant Lundquist," he said. "There's a problem over at the inn?"

The boy jumped to his feet. He was a good six-three, several inches taller than Fred. White, dark hair, brown eyes, big Adam's apple. He wore jeans and a T-shirt with a question mark of a man in a jumpsuit under a white hat.

"I didn't do it!" His voice verged on panic.

"Nobody says you did. What's your name, son?"

"Eddie. Eddie Stalcup."

"How old are you?"

"Eighteen. But I didn't do it!" He was holding it together. Just.

"Okay, Eddie, suppose we walk over there, and you can show me." He held the door.

"Show you what?"

"What you didn't do."

"Oh." Eddie looked around vaguely, a little calmer. "Just us?"

"For now. You can tell me about it on the way." He didn't wait for an answer.

Eddie followed him out. Fred set a pace that would stretch those long legs, maybe clear away some of the cobwebs.

"So, Eddie, what happened?"

"I don't know! One minute I was playing, and the next thing you know I was flat on my face. But I didn't grab those quilts. I know I didn't! And I didn't have anything to do with it. With her."

"Her? Who's that?"

"I don't know. The manager will tell you—she was there all the time!"

That could mean only one person. Fred girded himself for Mary Sue Ellett.

ELEVEN

Flat Iron

WHY IS IT taking so long?

Sitting on the floor, Joan was getting chilly. She tried not to look at the lumpy quilt, but her mind's eye saw the body under it flattened against the floor, like the possum she'd peeled off her sidewalk one morning.

From time to time she stood up, stretched, and looked over the railing. So far the orchestra was making remarkably little fuss.

She had called down to Alex when Eddie left, "There's a problem up here—Eddie's gone for help. He'll be right back."

To her relief, Alex had extended the break and she hadn't had to explain, much less ask the orchestra members to wait for the police. By now most of them had laid their instruments aside. Some were talking, some reading, some looking at the quilts around them. The percussionists were playing gin rummy across one of the timpani.

The doorframe dug into her back. Come on, Fred, she thought. This is your baby.

And then he was standing over her.

"Joan, what's wrong?"

"Fred, I'm so glad you're here." Her voice startled her by shaking. "I'm not used to this."

She reached up a hand. He pulled her to her feet and put an arm around her shoulders. His sweater felt warm, comforting.

"Used to what?"

Hadn't Eddie told him?

"It's Mary Sue." She pointed. "We found her like that."

Eddie was behind him. "I didn't do it!" he said.

"No, of course you didn't." Her own asperity quieted her shakes. "She's been here for hours."

Releasing her, Fred bent down and lifted the quilt by a corner. Joan looked again.

Except for the clear plastic bag clinging to her face, Mary Sue's body might have been laid out for viewing at Snarr's. The eyes were almost closed, and the right hand covered the left on her bosom. Her jaw sagged, though, and only the heavy makeup on her face and the bright red polish on her nails—if they were her nails—masked the pasty color of death. There was no condensation on the plastic, Joan noticed now. She wondered whether that meant anything.

Fred dropped the quilt.

"Did you touch her?" he asked.

Warmth rushed to her face. "Her foot," she said. "I touched her foot. I had to be sure."

Fred nodded. "How did you find her?"

"Eddie tripped in the dark, and there she was."

"You trip over the body?" he asked Eddie.

"No, over there," Eddie said, pointing to bare floorboards near it.

"Just tripped, is that it?"

"Yeah. And I didn't bring those quilts down with me, no matter what she thinks!" Eddie glared at Joan. "I didn't even touch 'em!"

"What were you doing up here in the first place?"

"It wasn't my idea," he said. "She made me do it. Because of the questions." Fred looked to Joan.

"He means the Charles Ives piece we were rehearsing," she said. "A distant trumpet plays a short theme that the flutes try to answer. We were up here trying to get Eddie far enough away from the orchestra to sound right. It worked fine. But he tripped in the dark. When I turned the lights on, we found her." She shrugged, feeling useless. "That's all I know."

"Anyone else been up here since then?"

"No. I sat in the doorway."

"What else did you touch besides the lights and her foot?"

"Just the quilt she was under. That's how we found her."

"Either one of you been up here before?"

"No," said Eddie.

"Yes," said Joan, remembering.

Fred raised his eyebrows.

"I came up yesterday, about half an hour after you let me in. The building had pretty well emptied out by then, but Mary Sue and her whole family were in here, hanging her mother's collection." She waved at the quilts that surrounded them. "I left before they did."

"Okay, we can get to that later," Fred said. "Let's get you out of here."

But instead of leaving, Eddie went back to the fireplace.

"Hey!" Fred said. "Come back here!"

"Just getting my trumpet." Eddie reached for the silver trumpet lying on the high mantel.

"Don't touch that!"

Eddie froze in mid-reach.

"How did it end up there?"

"I put it there." Injured innocence, but Eddie was right. Joan felt obliged to back him up.

"It's true, Fred. He was going to help me pick up the quilts on the floor. I did accuse him of bringing them down with him."

"Okay, Eddie. But you'll have to wait to take your horn until we're done in here." He herded them out of the room. "You two stay up here for now. And I don't want you discussing any of this with anyone. In a homicide, the less said, the better."

"Homicide!" said Eddie, his eyes wide. "You think someone killed her?"

"I don't know how she died."

"Could it be the plastic bag?" Joan asked, glad to be out of there. Was it the kind with printed warnings? She couldn't remember.

"I don't know," Fred said. "One thing's for sure. She didn't lay herself out like that."

"Not if she was already dead. But—" and Joan stopped herself. Mary Sue a suicide? Not the Mary Sue I know. And not the woman I saw last night. I don't believe it.

"Stay here, both of you. Don't let anyone else come up. I'll be right back."

Joan settled down on the floor outside the door. Eddie paced. This time the wait was much shorter. The first uniformed officer to arrive shooed them off. Politely. "Thank you, ma'am, but we're here now." She could imagine what Rebecca would have said.

THE PHOTOGRAPHER had started work when Sergeant Johnny Ketcham arrived. Fred was glad to see him. Ketcham was steady, reliable, and good with a crowd like the one downstairs. They worked well together.

"What've we got here?" Ketcham asked.

"I'm still not sure," Fred told him. "Take a look." He lifted the quilt that still covered the body. She'd been lying there a long time. The body fluids had pooled against the floor.

Ketcham pushed his wire-rims back against his nose. "How?"

"I don't know." Fred dropped the quilt.

"That doesn't hold a candle to the rest of those quilts," Ketcham said. "Looks more like the kind of thing my grandma used to make for the hired hands."

Ketcham would know. Five generations of Ketchams had lived in Indiana. Fred didn't think his own grandmother, a Swedish immigrant, would have known the difference.

"You call the coroner?" he asked. "And the state police?"

"On their way," Ketcham said.

Good. Sometimes Fred thought he spent most of his life waiting.

They waited for the state police lab technicians to roll back the quilt and peel off the plastic and waited again while the cameras flashed.

Dr. Henshaw arrived in sweatpants, probably straight from the Y. His body ran to a paunch. Lately, he'd taken to running to keep it off.

"Humph." Henshaw squatted effortlessly beside the body. "Help me turn her," he said. He needed the help. Mary Sue Ellett had been a hefty woman. Now, with rigor well established, she was a hefty stiff, and rolling her over her elbows onto her side was difficult.

Once they finally had her facedown, though, there was no question why she was dead. There were visible indentations in the back of her head.

"Sweet Jesus," Ketcham said reverently.

The cameras flashed again.

"That would do it," Fred said.

"No weapon?" Henshaw asked.

"She could have fallen on one of those wooden gizmos," Ketcham said.

"And dragged herself over here to die, with a plastic bag over her face?" Henshaw objected.

"Yeah." Fred looked around. There was plenty to look at—besides all the quilts, the room was full of old things. Most of the time the Sagamore Inn was a museum of sorts.

Maybe the Franklin stove? It was closer. But that head didn't look like a fall. It looked like more force than you'd see in a fall. No blood, though.

Then he saw it.

He had glanced at the mantelpiece when Eddie tried to claim his trumpet. But that was before he'd seen the back of Mary Sue's head. A blow like that would dent a trumpet, but this one was unmarred. Now the old-fashioned flatiron jumped out at him.

"How about that iron?" he asked. "Think it could do that much damage?"

Ketcham grinned.

"Are you kidding? My grandma Matlock kept on lifting those things on and off a coal stove in her kitchen long after the electricity reached their farm. She had muscles you wouldn't believe."

"The kid who found her parked his trumpet on the mantel," Fred said. "What do you want to bet he put the iron up there, too? Let's do a quick check on the people downstairs and then talk to him."

"Right."

Halfway down the stairs, Fred stopped. Sixty expectant faces turned up, and the hubbub died.

"Thank you for your patience," he said. "By now you may have guessed that there has been a death in the building. If you know anything at all about it, if you've been upstairs, or if you were here yesterday or today at any time before the rehearsal, we'll need to take your statements over at the police station. Otherwise, you're free to go. Please give your name and address and any information you might have to Sergeant Ketcham at the door."

"Who died?" someone shouted.

Fred held back. They'd know soon enough.

"We haven't reached the relatives yet," he said. "Sorry."

"Wait a minute, everybody!" No one was paying much attention to Joan, who was waving her hands in the air. "Don't go yet!" But they were packing up. The quickest among them were already heading for the door.

Fred blasted them with a two-fingered whistle that got their full attention, and then made the "all yours" gesture to Joan. Smiling her thanks, she climbed onto the podium.

"Alex asked me to ask you—can you all be here Saturday morning to finish this rehearsal?" A chorus of groans and moans objected. "Come on," she said. "It won't take long. How about if we start at ten? Anyone absolutely can't come?" Only a few bows waved in the air. "All right, then. See you here Saturday at ten sharp. And thanks." She stepped down.

"Any ringers here tonight?" Fred asked her.

"No, just the regulars. Here's a roster." She gave him a list of names, addresses, and phone numbers. "I marked all the ones who were here tonight."

"Thanks."

He stood back then and watched her check out music.

"OKAY, EDDIE," Fred said. They were sitting in what had been the first violin section. Behind Eddie, who was holding his trumpet like a baby, he could see Joan collecting abandoned music folders and unplugging extension cords and stand lights. "Tell me again about when you tripped."

"I told you. I just tripped."

"Over what?"

"I don't know. It was dark in there. Not—not her." He shuddered.

"You're sure?"

"Yeah, and I'm sure I didn't pull those quilts down!"

"Okay, okay. Think back. What did you feel when you hit the floor?"

"I didn't feel a darned thing. I was too mad. I thought I'd bent my horn."

"You had it in your hand when you fell?" Ketcham asked.

"Yeah. I went in there to play the question. I couldn't find the light switch. No problem—it's only five notes—and I could play them in the dark."

"Before you fell?"

"Yes. No. After. Both. I don't know. Ask Joan, why don't you?"

"We will," Fred said. "How about your other hand? You pick up anything?"

"No, I told you. Not until I started to pick up that cover."

"Maybe a pencil?" Ketcham asked. "Something you could have skidded on?"

"How many times do I have to say it?"

"Okay." Fred stood up. "Thanks, Eddie. Give us a call if you think of anything else. We'll be in touch. Meantime, don't talk about it. Not to anybody."

"That's it? I can go?"

"We'll need you to go over to the station to leave your fingerprints so we don't think they belong to a killer, and to put in writing what you just told us. Then you can go."

Eddie didn't wait for them to change their minds.

"THE LIGHTS HAVE just gone on," said Fred. He was sitting on the podium. Joan had taken the concertmaster's seat and would have been staring past him if her eyes hadn't been closed. "You're blinking a little. What do you see first?"

"Eddie. He's over by the fireplace. And his trumpet—it looks okay."

"Then what?"

"Quilts on the floor. You saw them. But I didn't know she was under them."

"What else?"

"The iron!" Her eyes popped open, and she leaned toward him. "Fred, that's it. There was an old-fashioned sadiron on the floor—you know, one of those heavy flat-irons they used to have to heat on a stove. That's what tripped Eddie! It was near Mary Sue's head—before I knew her head was there. I put in on the mantel."

Her face changed from delight to dismay.

"Oh, Fred. Is that—? Did it—?"

"Could be." He'd know soon.

"And I picked it up with both hands. Fred, I'm so sorry. I didn't know I was disturbing evidence."

"Can't be helped."

He sighed. Wondered where tonight's kids were. Wondered why nobody had looked into that room all day. He didn't need Henshaw to tell him the body had been there that long. And Joan had seen Mary Sue there the evening before. Had Mary Sue ever left?

"Think back to when you were here last night," he said. "What was it like in here?"

TWELVE

Scissors Chain

LAST NIGHT might as well be last year, Joan thought. Focus on the scene. How did it look? She turned her eyes from the walls hung with quilts to the plain one opposite her.

In her mind the Elletts gathered, and with them, some of the rest of it.

"There were two big stepladders," she said. "And bags on the floor."

She wound the cord around a stand light and laid it with the others in the box at her feet.

Fred nodded and handed her another light.

"What kind of bags?" asked Ketcham.

Plastic garbage bags. She didn't have to think about that. "This place was crawling with them yesterday. There were plenty in that room. Some still had quilts in them."

"You could see through them?" Ketcham sounded as if he didn't care.

"Yes." And through him. "Just like the plastic on her face."

Fred looked tired. He reached for a light and slowly, deliberately, began wrapping its cord around it.

"The committee specified either marked pillowcases or clear plastic, Johnny, so no one would toss out a quilt with the garbage. Or sneak two out in one big bag." He tucked the plug into the end of the coiled cord.

"So Mary Sue's killer was there before they put the bags away," Joan said. Does that mean it's a member of the family?

"Or knew where they put them," said Fred. "Or brought one along."

Of course. Why don't I keep my big mouth shut? She wound another light.

"What about the iron?"

She stared into the box of lights but had to shake her head.

"I don't remember it. I wasn't looking at the floor then."

"Who was there last night?" he asked.

"In the room?"

"For starters."

"Mary Sue, of course. Her sister and brother. Her sister's husband. And the cousin who took care of Edna, Mary Sue's mother, before she died."

"Just family?"

"Yes. They were hanging Edna's quilt collection in that room. I don't think the judges were going to have anything to do with it."

"Leon Ellett's still local," Ketcham put in.

"Alice doesn't live here anymore," Joan said, and felt silly. What was that, anyway? A song? A movie? She plowed on. "She came back for her mother's funeral. Her husband is Harold somebody. I didn't get his last name. Kitty Graf—that's the cousin—talked about wanting to stay on in Edna's house." She shook her head. "I don't know how that will turn out now." Or how it would have turned out with Mary Sue alive, for that matter. A strange family, what's left of it.

"Will you go back in there with us and look around?" Fred asked. "Tell us what's changed, or whatever else you notice."

Rebecca or no Rebecca, Joan put the last light in the box and went.

Halfway up one curving stairway, she was relieved to see the stretcher start down the other, its burden covered with something she couldn't see through. Her shoulders dropped tension she hadn't known was there.

The room looked different now. She wondered what the police hoped to learn from the quilts they were examining on the floor. One man was actually vacuuming them.

"Hey, Fred," another man said. "Look at this."

Squatting beneath a bare pole, he was pointing to a little pair of scissors at the base of one wooden support. Stork-shaped scissors.

"Oh!" It slipped out.

Fred turned toward her.

"Something wrong?"

Silly question, she thought, under the circumstances. But she knew what he meant.

"Fred, those look like Edna's scissors. I saw them when we were working on the orchestra quilt. You'll probably find a needle and thread, too. Kitty brought them that day. Last night they used them when they were sewing Edna's quilts to the cloth they put the poles through—like curtain rods."

They went over to an old one that was still hanging. It gave Joan the willies to imagine piecing its postage-stamp-size bits together, much less quilting them. Basted to one corner was a neat cloth label dating it to 1850 and attributing it to a Berry ancestor who must have had a lot of time on her hands.

"Eddie says he didn't pull them down," Fred said. "The lab can probably tell whether the threads were cut or broken." He turned to Ketcham. "Be sure Henshaw sees the scissors. Ask him to check her for cuts."

Ketcham nodded, wrote something down, and went over to the pole.

Cuts? A struggle? Small as they were, the stork-shaped scissors were sharp enough, Joan knew. But she had heard a different kind of struggle. Whispered words swam to the surface of her memory: "She'd never leave it to you!" and "I'll stop you. You have no right!"

"They've rearranged the quilts since last night," she said slowly.

"The ones on the floor?"

She wished she could raise one eyebrow like that. Was Fred pulling her leg? Never mind.

"When I came up last night, that big Double Wedding Ring against the wall was blocking the door. I could hear people whispering on the other side of it, but I couldn't tell who they were. At the time I figured it wasn't any of my business. But now..."

And she told him.

"OKAY, FRED SAID. "Let's go over this again." They were back down in Snarr's chairs. "The family doesn't know what was in the old lady's will. Kitty wants the house. Leon's hurting for cash. Alice doesn't approve of Leon or anybody, including Mary Sue."

Joan nodded.

"That about got it?"

"Except for the notes."

"Notes?"

Sorry, Kitty, she thought. Sorry Edna. "We found a note in the orchestra quilt after Edna worked on it."

"A note." This time both eyebrows rose. "To you?"

"No, to Edna. Her memory went bad before she died. Kitty had started writing her reminders about all kinds of ordinary things, and she says Edna hated them. She hid those notes—and who knows what else? Kitty was trying to keep it secret. I don't know how much the family knew." *I kept it from Leon, but I have to tell Fred. Don't I?*

"We'll talk to Kitty." He yawned. "And the rest of them."

Joan caught his yawn and tried to read her watch. Her eyes were slow to focus. Half past nine. It felt more like midnight.

"What time did you leave them?"

"Around six. They still had a lot to do."

"And they were the only ones in the building?"

"I think so." Then she remembered her run-in with Catherine, hesitated, and knew she was caught.

I don't want to tell him all that. But I've waited too long. Now no matter what I say, he'll think I'm covering something up. And he'll be right.

"No," she said firmly. "When I came down here after I left them, I ran into the caterer. She was just starting to set up for a reception this afternoon. These chairs had blocked her path. We worked it out."

He didn't push it. Maybe he was too tired. He probably already knew Catherine was catering the show. Or could find out. How many caterers did Oliver have, anyway? But Catherine and the Elletts weren't the only ones in the inn when she left, were they?

"Fred, didn't the kids who spent the night hear something?"

"You see 'em?" A question for an answer.

"No." How could she have missed them? And why didn't he know? "The Elletts were in the only upstairs room with light showing. I thought they were you and the kids."

"How long did the fellow who brought the chairs stay?"

"He took off when we finished setting up. Before I went upstairs. It was quiet by then."

"Did you watch him leave the building?" That was Ketcham.

"No, he knew his way." Come on. You think Bud Snarr sent him over to create a little extra business?

"So he could have let someone in," Ketcham persisted. Oh.

"So could a lot of people," she said. "Catherine, the Elletts—they all left after the dragon with the checklist went home."

An uneasiness settled at the base of her skull. Usually that meant she was missing something. She had learned to slow down and wait for a clear look at whatever it was— her keys in the ignition, the black nine she could move to a red ten in solitaire. Tonight she couldn't see a thing, but the feeling persisted. She tried listening.

Not a sound after her parting shot to Catherine. Afraid of saying something she wouldn't be able to live with later, she had walked away and closed the big door softly. Silently.

Too silently.

"The door! I pulled it shut, but I'm sure the lock didn't catch. Fred, it's my fault!" And you trusted me.

"Don't give it a thought. You weren't the last. Besides, you saw how well your dragon watched that door during the day."

Right, buried in bags of quilts.

"Anyone could have slipped past her while it was so noisy."

"And hung around," Fred said.

It was spooky enough at night in that old building. Had she been there with a killer lying in wait? Joan shivered. In wait for Mary Sue, or would just anyone have done? Had she escaped a random killer by pure luck? What if she had set up later? And what if—

"What if he's still here?"

"No such luck. Our guys searched. Nobody here but us chickens."

She worked at believing it. He did mean to kill Mary Sue, she thought, and he succeeded. Of course. Why hang around?

"You all right?" Fred's arm warmed her shoulder again.

"Thanks, Fred." She pulled herself together. "If you're done with me, I think I'd better take this stuff home. I had to sign my name in blood to get the lights."

"They should be safe enough here now. We've posted a police guard."

Locking the barn door, and all that. But she didn't say it. He was looking too grim.

"You think the killer might come back?"

"Don't know. Depends on a lot of things. Like whether he got what he came for."

"She's dead."

"But the quilts are still here, except the few we took as evidence."

"Fred, that's crazy. Why would anyone kill to steal quilts? Why not haul them off when no one's around?"

"Suppose you plan to do just that. You wait in the building until everyone leaves. And then she surprises you by coming back while you're cutting them down. Maybe you strike out with those little scissors, but they don't stop her. So you clobber her with the nearest heavy object—the iron on the mantel.''

Ketcham was nodding.

"Not bad. It fits.''

It would take a lot to stop Mary Sue, Joan thought. But wait a minute.

''Why do all that and leave all the quilts?''

''Panic,'' said Ketcham. ''Or he didn't leave them all.''

''We don't have an inventory,'' Fred said.

''Yes, you do,'' said Joan. ''Or you will. When I arrived here yesterday, they were rushing a last-minute list of all Edna's quilts to the printer for the program. Mary Sue was still alive and kicking then—she sent the list down. Besides, I saw her after that.''

''Good.'' Now Fred's eyes were smiling with the rest of his face. ''Now let's get you over to the station to put it in writing.''

But she wasn't on foot this time. Rats.

''My car's here, Fred—I'm going to take the extra music and stuff with me, guard or no guard.''

''I'll be right back, Johnny.''

She thanked him for helping her carry the boxes out to the car—probably all he meant in the first place—and drove the half-block to the police station. That feeling at the base of her skull was reaching her back teeth.

THIRTEEN

Johnny-Around-the-Corner

WHEN FRED GOT BACK, Ketcham had the kids.

"Where'd you find them?"

"I didn't. They just got here. Root, here, had the good sense to bring them in."

Fred nodded at the rookie officer, a stocky blonde. Evidently she was smart enough to listen to kids.

"They say anything?"

"No, sir. Not really. But they wouldn't leave—said you wanted them inside. I thought I'd better ask."

"Thanks. Keep using your head out there."

"Yes, sir." She left unobtrusively, and he turned his attention to the kids.

There were four of them, two boys and two girls. The boys were leaning against the wall as if they crossed police barriers every day, but their enlarged pupils gave away their true feelings. The girls, just as big-eyed, weren't even pretending.

He'd already forgotten their names.

Mary Sue had refused to spring for an off-duty cop. Instead, she'd recruited the children of her committee members. Patiently, Fred had instructed them. Last night they'd settled in with soft drinks and sleeping bags, treating the whole thing as a big lark. He thought he'd left them very clear about their responsibilities—and about calling for help instead of challenging an intruder. But they hadn't called.

And why were they showing up late tonight?

"We're not late," said the boy who was tall enough to make a basketball coach smile. Maybe he did. Not knowing who was on the team branded Fred an outsider. Ketcham, like any real Hoosier, would know the local starting five cold. "She told us they'd be rehearsing till ten."

"Miss Ellett didn't see any point in us hanging around while the orchestra was here," one of the girls explained.

Wonderful. Mary Sue had meddled with their security plans, such as they were, but hadn't thought fit to tell him. He could cheerfully have killed her—except someone had beaten him to it.

"And last night? After I saw you?"

"Last night?" The girl's eyes opened even wider. "Is that when it happened? I didn't hear a thing—nothing like a fight or a shot or anything." She turned to the other three. "Did you guys?"

"No," said the shorter boy, who sported a mustache and an earring. "And we weren't goofing off, either. We took turns making the rounds about every half hour—in pairs, like you said. Checked all the doors."

"Went in all the upstairs rooms?"

"Yeah. Flashed a light around and everything. We didn't see anybody."

"That's right." Heads bobbed in earnest unison.

"Nobody? You're sure?"

"Not after the Elletts went home. They stayed pretty late. We didn't bother them once we found out who was in there."

"You never checked that room again?"

The boy with the mustache stroked his upper lip, as if for comfort. The girls stared at the floor.

They were only kids. What could he say?

KETCHAM WAS DRIVING. He hung a left at the high school.

"How you want to break it to 'em?"

"With our eyes open." Fred leaned his head back against the doorframe and felt his own lids droop. He was getting too old for all-nighters.

Ketcham's wire-rims reflected the dim green light of the dashboard clock. Past ten—it felt more like two. "You'd think somebody would have missed her by now."

"Not me." Fred grinned. "But you're right. They had all kinds of stuff scheduled at the inn today."

They made a pit stop on the way to Edna Ellett's house. In the men's room, Fred's pocket beeped. Something too sensitive for the radio monitored by police scanners all over town. He fished for a quarter and headed for the outdoor pay phone.

"I'm putting you through to the captain," the dispatcher said. "Good luck."

Just enough warning. Fred tilted the receiver away to protect his hearing.

"Fred, what in blue blazes have you been doing!"

He knew better than to answer. The veins on Warren Altschuler's neck had to be standing out.

"I give you a simple little security job. And what do you do? You palm it off on children—and let it turn into a homicide!"

Fred held his tongue.

"Now the chief's raking *me* over for putting the mayor's daughter in danger."

"Deckard's daughter?" Fred groaned inwardly. He'd never made the connection. Oliver was full of Deckards.

Altschuler's voice turned sweet. "His only one. The very apple of his eye." Then he bellowed again. "Dammit, Fred, what am I supposed to tell him?"

"I don't know." An imp overtook him. "I suppose you could say I don't think she did it."

"You *what?*"

"Look, Warren, if you need ammunition, try this: Those kids spent all last night in the building. We can't rule them out, no matter whose kids they are. But the mayor's got a point. Someone may think they know more than they do. You want to take them into protective custody?"

"You aren't serious." Altschuler's steam was cooling.

"I'm dead serious." In the back of Fred's head, his own words were reminding him who else might appear to know too much. "He could at least tell them to keep their mouths shut."

"Report to me tonight."

"Yes, sir."

Back in the car, he risked shutting his eyes for a moment. No danger now of falling asleep—his pulse was pounding against his ribs and in his ears. Murder he could handle; it was the politics that tore him up. He fought his shallow breathing. In . . . out . . . in . . . out . . . in . . . out. . . .

He blinked to alertness when Ketcham said, "We're here."

Two cars filled the short driveway to Edna Ellett's big old house, and light shone through the bay window. At least someone was up. It was worse when you had to wake them.

Ketcham eased Fred's Chevy to the curb and spoke into the radio.

Fred dreaded death notifications. The Elletts would be facing their second death in what—a week? And this one was murder. With energy born of anger, he climbed the limestone steps and touched the bell. Through beveled glass panes beside the door he saw a large figure loom larger.

"Leon," Ketcham murmured. He straightened his lapels, and then the door opened.

Fred took in the square jaw and bushy brows. Translate Mary Sue into a man, he thought, and you'd have her brother, with a good three inches and fifty pounds on me.

"Hiya, Johnny," Leon said to Ketcham. He held the door wide. "Come on in. What's up?"

Johnny, huh? Fred tagged after him into a large front hall.

"Hey, Alice," Leon boomed back into the recesses of the house. "It's Johnny Ketcham." If Leon knew, he was covering well. Beaming welcome, he led them through an arched doorway into a living room full of antiques and Oriental rugs. The place smelled old—floor wax mingled with mildew.

A small-boned woman dwarfed by coils of her own dark hair promptly appeared under a second arch. Even in miniature, Mary Sue's eyebrows and jaw were unmistakable. Alice's plain, scrubbed face lit up with what looked like genuine pleasure.

"Johnny!" She came toward them, holding out her hand. "It's so good to see you again. How's your mother?"

"Pretty good, Alice, but she doesn't get out much. I'll tell her you asked."

"Maybe I can get over to visit her while I'm home."

"She'd like that." He released her hand, took a step backward, and shut his mouth.

Alice and Leon were standing on a plush Chinese floral rug and Fred and Ketcham on a threadbare Bokhara a lot like one Linda Lundquist had spent a bundle on just before she left Fred.

The rugs clashed. The whole room clashed, but it had that lived-in look, with papers overflowing a cherry rolltop, rings marring the marble tables at the end of the sofa, and charred logs in the carved limestone fireplace. The old lady had probably inherited a lot of the stuff herself. Now the next generation was Johnny-on-the-spot to divvy it up again. All but Mary Sue, of course.

"Good of you both to come by," Leon said. "Mom thought a lot of you, Johnny. What'll you drink? And your friend? I didn't get the name."

Not waiting for it, Alice slid onto a brocade love seat that rocked in a mahogany frame, almost like a garden swing.

"Do sit down," she said.

Fred stayed on his feet and watched Ketcham straighten the legs that had started lowering him into a high-backed maple rocker. "I'm Lieutenant Fred Lundquist, Oliver Police."

Alice's lips tightened, and a clear voice broke in.

"What are you doing here?"

From the hall, a woman was staring at them over the stair railing. Bare toes under a fleecy wraparound. This had to be the cousin.

"It's all right, Kitty," Alice called through the archway. "Come meet Johnny Ketcham's lieutenant. You remember Johnny."

"I don't think so," Kitty said, but she padded into the living room. Alice stood to introduce her.

"This is our cousin, Kitty Graf. She's been living with Mother." Ketcham shook hands.

As small and dark as Alice, Kitty didn't resemble her otherwise. Her chin came to a point, and her brows were thin lines. At first glance, he had put her age at forty, but up close the dark circles under sagging eyes added at least ten years.

Fred reached down to take the small warm hand she offered. Short nails polished a medium shade—she'd probably wear makeup during the day—a strong handshake.

"Fred Lundquist."

She nodded and turned those eyes on him. Were their shadows caused by grief or nothing more than windy days and spring trees? Southern Indiana supported more than its share of allergists.

"What are you doing here?" she asked again.

This was the part he hated. There wasn't any good way.

"I wish I didn't have to tell you. We've come with bad news—the worst kind." He paused to let them take that much in.

"It's Mary Sue." He waited again—sometimes that was enough—but this group didn't jump in. So he had to say it. "I'm very sorry. A terrible thing has happened, and Mary Sue is dead."

"Dead!" burst from Leon, and "Mary Sue? Dead?" from Alice.

"Dead," Kitty said in an empty voice. "Edna's dead." She sat down mechanically on the nearest chair. Leon didn't move.

Alice groped her way back to the love seat. "Mary Sue?" she said again. "I can't believe it. Are you sure, Johnny? Maybe they mixed up the bodies." Good old denial.

"No, Alice," said Ketcham softly. "I'm awful sorry. It's Mary Sue and no mistake."

Fred paused again. "We know this must be a shock to you, and we regret having to disturb you with formalities at a time like this. But even though we're sure, we need to ask a family member to make the formal identification."

"Don't worry, little Alice," said Leon. "I'll do it." And then, "My God, Johnny, can't you even keep the drunks off the road on a weeknight?"

"This was no accident." Ketcham's feathers didn't ruffle easily—one of the things Fred appreciated most about this middle-aged sergeant.

"Not an accident? But Johnny, she wouldn't kill herself!" Alice's voice rose. "Not Mary Sue!"

"We don't think she did." Ketcham slid his eyes over to Fred and caught his nod. "It looks as if she was murdered." The word soaked into the rugs.

Alice recovered first.

"Murdered! How? Why? Was it a burglar?"

"We're not sure yet," Fred said. "We're just beginning our investigation."

"It must have been. Who else would kill Mary Sue?"

"That's what we'll be working to find out. I take it no enemies jump to mind."

"Oh, no!" She shocked easily. He gentled it.

"Maybe someone who resented her."

"I can't imagine who."

Fred searched her face. Either she lacked imagination, or she didn't know her sister as well as he did. Or she *did* know—that, and more. Was she fooling herself or trying to fool him? It wasn't time to push.

"What about that fellow she used to be married to?" Ketcham asked.

"He died a few years after the divorce," Leon said. "Good riddance."

"Did she have children?" Fred asked. Johnny Ketcham probably knew.

"No," Alice said. "She said she didn't want them, but I think it was that man. When he left her, she was so strong and brave about it. She threw herself into good causes.

We're—we're all the family she had." She sniffed a little and poked around in a pocket, but her hands came up as empty as her eyes were dry.

So you'd inherit, Fred thought.

"Do you know if she'd made a will?"

"Not much point," Leon said. "About all she had was the house. She was living pretty close to the bone."

Leon had probably tried to touch her for a loan.

"She still work at the college?"

"Yeah, Johnny. And you know how it is. Not much chance for a raise—they can always get people with kids."

Ketcham bailed Fred out.

"They promise free tuition—here, or to any college in the country, up to Oliver's tuition. It's a good deal for big families, but it shoots hell out of the labor market. Pardon me, Alice."

Fred nodded and sat down in a cherry side chair next to a marble-topped table. Ketcham finally sank into the rocker.

"She'd have her share of Mother's estate," Alice said suddenly. "I'm sure Mother left a will."

"Oh, come on, Alice," said Leon, resting an elbow on the mantelpiece. "We've turned the place upside down, but we haven't found any will. And we're not going to—because it doesn't exist. I asked Mom a dozen times before she died. She couldn't remember writing any will."

Kitty nodded sadly. "There was a lot she couldn't remember."

"That doesn't mean she didn't." Alice glared at Leon.

"It doesn't mean she did." He straightened up and glared back.

Like a couple of kids, Fred thought. He had a sudden image of the two of them, much younger, duking it out in this very room.

"You grow up in this house?"

"No," said Kitty.

"Yes," said Leon and Alice simultaneously. That did it; tears came streaming down Alice's face. She let them fall, only clearing her eyes with a bare finger.

"Oh, Leon," she wailed. "First Mama, now Mary Sue. We're the only ones left."

Leon crossed the room to stand behind her, his big hands covering her shoulders. He stared over her head at Ketcham.

"Johnny, you got to get him! Whatever it takes."

A good time to take charge. Fred turned his good-cop face toward Leon.

"Thank you, Mr. Ellett. We'll do our best not to make it any more painful than it has to be."

Kitty stared at him with those eyes. Alice pulled herself together again.

"When—when did it happen?"

"Right now we're not even sure of that. Did you see her today?"

"No. She didn't live with Mother, you know. We've been trying to sort things out here, but Mary Sue's been spending half her life over at the inn."

As it turned out, all the rest of it, Fred thought.

"And yesterday?" he asked.

"We were all working together over there last night until almost midnight. Even my husband helped—he went to bed early tonight."

"Working?"

"Hanging Edna's quilts." Kitty made it sound like trampling the flag.

"Edna was our mother," Alice explained. She had herself well in hand now.

"That late?" Fred wondered what the kids had logged, if they'd remembered to log anything. He scribbled "12? log?" in his notebook.

"Oh, sure. Mary Sue's a real slave driver, and a hellion if you cross her."

"Leon!"

"Sorry, little Alice. Guess it hasn't sunk in yet. What happened?"

Fred ducked it for the moment. "She was found tonight during the orchestra's dress rehearsal. We'll know more when we get the coroner's report."

"The orchestra?" Alice sounded blank. "Why on earth ... ?"

"They were over at the inn tonight—they're going to play for the opening on Sunday." Maybe. If there even is an opening. "You were working there together last night. I suppose you all left together." He didn't mean it as a question.

"No," said Kitty.

"Yes," said Alice.

They looked at each other.

"Don't say another word," Leon told them. "Not until I call a lawyer."

"Go ahead, if you think you should," said Ketcham. "We'll even get one for you if you're hard up. You don't have to talk to us at all, you can always stop talking, and anything you tell us can be used in court. Do what you think you should. But Leon, you said it yourself. We've got to get him. There's a killer out there."

Or in here, Fred thought.

FOURTEEN

Boy's Nonsense

JOAN WALKED INTO a blessedly quiet house. Propped up against the toaster was a note from Andrew: "Out with R—don't wait up."

You bet. I'm not going to justify myself to anyone at this hour.

Relieved, she climbed the stairs, peeled off her clothes, fastened her hair up out of the way, and stepped into the hottest shower she could stand, letting it pound her shoulders and the fingers that still remembered that cold foot. With a rough towel she rubbed the old skin off her own warm feet and ankles, ignoring the beginnings of stubble on her shins and calves. A clean, sun-dried nightgown— the first of the season—smelled sweet going over her head.

I'll never fall asleep, she thought drowsily. She crawled into bed and opened *Van Loon's Lives,* an old standby in times of stress.

After a while, familiar voices registered somewhere in her brain, but sleep had already glued her eyes shut. She didn't feel the book slip from her fingers or hear it hit the floor.

HER READING LIGHT was still burning—faintly now in the morning sun that flooded the room. Joan lay in bed, more than usually tempted to pull the covers over her head and shut out the world. But the smell of coffee brewed by someone else was irresistible. Reaching over her head, she

turned off the light. Then she rolled over and rescued Van
Loon.

Down in the kitchen, they were devouring the headlines
with breakfast. They didn't look up when she came in.

"I'm telling you, Rebecca, you can't trust her for a
minute." Andrew kept a straight face.

"You don't think she did it herself!"

"Mom?" He caught a toaster waffle on the fly. "After
last fall, I wouldn't put it past her—oh, hi, Mom." It was
an exaggerated double take.

"Morning, you two." She poured herself a bowl of granola, a glass of skim milk, and a cup of black coffee.

"Good rehearsal last night?" Andrew asked inno-
cently.

Rebecca dropped the nonsense. "What really happened?"

"What does the paper say?" Joan sat down beside Andrew and sipped the coffee.

"Not much, actually," said Andrew. "Serves 'em right
for going morning. They didn't have time to get it all in."

"They say you found a dead woman at the Sagamore
Inn—and the police think she was murdered. Nothing
about why they think so. Your Captain Altschuler's not
what I'd call talkative."

"Who?"

"Isn't that your cop?"

"Rebecca, he's not my cop. And his name isn't Altschuler." Joan reached for the paper. "Good Lord."

She hadn't seen the camera, but there she was on page
one, staring straight into it. Beside her, Fred was hefting
the box of orchestra music folders into her trunk. She
supposed it could have been worse—a moment earlier he'd
had an arm around her. As it was, the caption writer
hadn't identified his bent back. She got full billing—both

as the manager of the Oliver Civic Symphony and as the woman who had found the body of Mary Sue Ellett. No mention of Eddie. Or of last year's orchestra murders.

The paper's lead story boosted the quilt show, but with only one small photo, and that was of Mary Sue.

Bet I bumped a quilt off the front page, Joan thought.

"So who got it this time, Mom? What did you know about her?"

"Andrew, don't be such a ghoul."

"It's all right, Rebecca. I'd better get used to it." Joan knew it was true. "I'm amazed the phone hasn't been ringing off the hook."

"It can't." Rebecca grinned. "After it woke me at six, I turned off the bell."

"So?" Andrew drowned another bite of waffle in an outrageous pool of syrup. Joan took a deep breath.

"She was in charge of the quilt show and a member of the orchestra board. She meant well enough, and she really did a lot of good, but she tended to bulldoze people."

"This is a victim? Pass the butter, Bec."

Rebecca passed it. "Maybe someone who'd had it with her lay in wait and stabbed her when the orchestra would cover her screams."

"And you call *me* a ghoul." He slathered butter on another waffle.

"Stop it!"

Their banter was suddenly too much to bear. So was the prospect of going to work. The only difference there would be the tone of the questions—and her relation to the questioners.

"I'm sorry, Mom." Andrew gave her a sticky hug. "I keep forgetting that it's real. And that you were really there."

"Me, too." Rebecca reached across the table to place a hand on hers.

"Thanks. I didn't mean to yell. Guess I'm not as tough as I thought I was."

"Tell me about the show, Mom." Rebecca patted her hand and changed the subject with studied casualness. "Did you see any of the quilts?"

"Rebecca! How could I forget? Yours is great!"

"You *saw* it?" Nothing casual about that. "Where?"

"In the big room where the orchestra's going to play—right by the violas, would you believe that? My stand partner couldn't keep his hands off her bottom."

"You didn't let him!"

"I didn't know it was yours. Besides, I don't know what I could have done to stop him—he didn't exactly ask. I don't think he hurt her any."

Andrew was staring at her. Rebecca grinned.

"Let him wonder, Mom."

"He'll love it," Joan said. "Only I don't know when anyone will be allowed back in that building."

"Because of the murder?" Andrew asked.

"Yes." She sat quietly for a moment, willing it not to have happened, but reality pushed back into her mind. It wasn't real, though, she thought. She could see the face waiting under its transparent cover—almost like the fairy tale, she thought suddenly. But someone's twisted it into Sleeping Ugly. She shivered.

And then she knew what she had to tell Fred.

She pushed back her chair, mumbled an apology through her last spoonful of granola, and bolted for the upstairs phone. Behind her, she could hear Andrew.

"I don't know, Rebecca. I just live here."

With her bedroom door closed, Joan dialed the police. No, she couldn't speak to Lieutenant Lundquist—would she like to leave a message? She wouldn't, but she did, torn between not wanting to have to deal with a stranger and knowing that waiting to speak to Fred himself would only decrease the likelihood that anything she might say would help.

To her astonishment, her name was an open sesame.

"Could you hang on just a minute, ma'am? Let me check."

Maybe I should hit the news more often, she thought—but there have to be easier ways.

"Lundquist." His fatigue came through in only one word. No wonder they were screening his calls.

"Fred, it's Joan."

"Are you all right?"

Bless you, she thought. Not did I think of something to solve your murder. Just am I all right. I do like this man.

"A lot better than last night. But you sound worn out."

"I'll survive. What's up?"

For a moment, she'd blocked it out.

"Just a thought, but you said to call if I thought of anything."

"Sure."

"Last night, we had it all figured out. Someone came in to steal quilts and got caught. In a panic, he attacked Mary Sue and took off."

"Mmm."

"So who laid her out?"

"Yeah. And why?" Of course he'd thought of it. She felt silly. But why stop now?

"For that matter, why was the room so different?"

"Different?" He came alive. "What was different?"

"You probably know that, too," she backpedaled. "There was the stuff on the floor, of course. Some of the other quilts had been moved. And those big ladders were gone—I'm sure I told you that. The whole place was colder and emptier."

"Mmm." His voice sounded bored, but she could hear his pencil scratching faintly.

She risked a question.

"Did you see the Elletts? Is it all public knowledge now?"

"I told them—but not everything."

"What does that mean?"

"The less information people have about the murder scene, the easier it will be for the murderer to give himself away by saying something most folks wouldn't know. So don't talk about it. Not to anybody."

"Sure. Fred, how were they?"

"Hard to tell. They didn't fall apart."

"I wouldn't expect them to. You should have heard them in the funeral parlor after their mother died."

"Oh?" Those eyebrows, she thought, wishing she could see them in person. "They raise a ruckus?"

"Not that bad. Or maybe it was. They kept getting in subtle digs all around. A real fight would have been easier to take. I'll tell you, Fred, I was glad to get out of there— the open casket was the least of it."

"Uh-huh." He sounded tired again. "Anything else?"

"No. Fred, I'm sorry. I didn't want to bother you—"

He stopped her.

"All I don't need is to miss something because you don't want to bother me with it." She felt better. "Call me anytime. Just don't spread it around."

"I won't."

IT HAD SOUNDED EASY. But by the time the orchestra president called at noon to ask her to visit the Elletts with sympathy gifts of flowers and food, she thought, almost anything would be easier than staying at work. The office phone, which she couldn't ignore, and the senior citizens themselves had worn her down. Still, she hesitated.

"It just doesn't feel right for me to be the one."

"Nonsense. You'll do it beautifully, and I'm sure the family will appreciate the chance to talk to you."

That's what I'm worried about, Joan thought. They're going to want to hear the stuff I've been trying all day not to tell anybody.

But she already knew she'd go.

It's only being neighborly, she thought on the way to Edna's house. After all, Mary Sue had her good points, and I can't help liking Leon some of the time. Kitty, bless her, took care of Edna. As for Alice—who knows what she'll be like when Mary Sue isn't breathing down her neck?

Standing on the porch with the orchestra's baked ham in one hand and spring flowers in the other (by not telling the Flower Basket they were for a death in the family she had succeeded in coming away with irises and tulips instead of gladiolus and carnations), she could hear them shouting.

I don't need this, she thought.

Neither did Mary Sue, a tougher part of her answered. Go in there and listen. Maybe you'll learn something.

FIFTEEN

Battleground

SHE HAD TO RING the bell a second time. Then the silence was abrupt.

Kitty opened the door, looking appropriately somber. A thirties-style cotton apron covered most of her black turtleneck and gray slacks.

"Won't you come in?" she said. "The family's in the living room."

Like the apron, old photographs in the hallway reminded Joan of Edna. Could that one be her wedding portrait? she wondered. And who is this baby—Mary Sue? Leon? I wish I'd visited when she could have told me.

"You've got company," Kitty was saying. She waved Joan into the living room ahead of her.

Wearing calling-hour clothes and smooth faces that Joan didn't believe in for a moment, Alice and Leon rose to greet her.

"I hope I'm not interrupting," she said, sure that she was. "The symphony board asked me to express their sympathy. What a terrible, terrible thing!"

She held out the orchestra's gifts. Kitty came forward, and Joan loaded her down with the ham and spring flowers.

Leon crushed her hand in his big paw.

"It's good to see you, again, little Joan." He beamed down at her. "Thank you for coming." She was suddenly glad she had agreed to go, if it meant something to him.

She got only a perfunctory handshake from his sister, though. Skipping the niceties, Alice went right to the point.

"The paper said you found her. Is that true?"

Dear God.

"Well, yes and no."

Alice's eyes flashed. "Mary Sue was my sister!"

"Another member of the orchestra saw her first," Joan said carefully. "But I was there, and I was the person on the scene when the police arrived."

"What happened? They won't say a word!"

"I don't know. I wish I could tell you more, but I can't." Because I promised, she thought. But when it came right down to it, it was true—she couldn't. She didn't even know for sure what had killed Mary Sue, much less who.

I could probably make a stab at when, though, she thought, remembering the cold, rigid flesh under her fingers. I'll bet anything nobody saw her all day yesterday. Question is, did she come in early, or was she killed the night before?

"You at least know what she looked like!" Now tears glistened. Was it possible that Alice really cared? "Nobody will tell me anything!"

"Alice, her face wasn't touched," Leon said. "I saw her, remember? Why won't you believe me?"

If Leon had seen the body, what harm could there be in confirming the comfort he was handing out?

"That's true," Joan said. She supposed they could even have another open-casket funeral.

"Was she—attacked?"

Murdered isn't attacked? Just in time, Joan resisted blurting it out. And the red rising to Alice's cheeks made plain what she couldn't bring herself to say.

"Goodness, Alice, I don't think so." Not with those skintight pants still on, anyhow. "Not that I'd know," she added quickly.

With every evasion, she was becoming more uncomfortable. I never should have said yes to this, she thought. I knew better. She turned to Kitty, who was still holding the flowers in one hand and the supermarket's aluminum platter of baked ham in the other.

"Could I help you with those?" The ham weighed a good five pounds, she knew.

"I can do it," said Kitty, her hands steady. "I did for Edna."

"Be careful with the vase!" Alice warned. "I know her," she said to Joan, as if Kitty had already left the room. "She'll put those irises into Mother's antique Chinese vase—and who knows how much it's worth by now?"

The knuckles whitened on the fist that held the irises.

"Flags," Kitty said. "Edna called them flags. And she trusted me with her things. Who do you think always dusted the vase you're all of a sudden so worried about?" Without waiting for an answer, she marched out, flags waving.

Alice whirled on her brother.

"Did you hear that, Leon? She's staking her claim. You *knew* she wanted the house—now she's making her move on Mother's beautiful things."

"Calm down, Alice." The high tenor voice came from behind Joan. Turning, she saw Alice's husband holding a pencil over an honest-to-goodness clipboard. "Nobody's getting anything until it's all been appraised."

"Oh, Harold, you don't understand!" Alice wailed.

"I understand that you're upset. But there's no need to get hysterical. The court is going to want to see your mother's things divided fairly—or sold, and the proceeds distributed to you and Leon. Kitty won't get a thing. I've explained all that to you."

"I'm losing my whole family, and all you can think about is money. This isn't about money!" Her voice shook, and her eyes, though dry, were wild.

"Speak for yourself, Alice," Leon said. "But you don't need to, do you? You can mouth all that family bull because you know old money-grubbing Harold will never let you miss out on a penny that's coming to you."

"I resent that!" Harold laid the clipboard on the mantel and looked ready to square off. "Especially from you. You know that what's good for Alice is in your interest, too."

Joan wished she was invisible. No such luck. Leon reached for her hand and pulled her over. She felt like a human shield.

"Joan, meet Harold Franklin—Alice's husband. Harold, this is Joan Spencer. She brought flowers from one of Mary Sue's good works."

"And she knew Mother," Alice put in. Regaining her composure now, she smiled at her husband. "Harold's a CPA, Joan. He's really a great help. It's all so complicated, what with Mary Sue going before we knew what was hers."

"We met the other night," Joan said. They shook hands. Trying to remember what Leon had told her about slow lawyers, and hoping she wasn't plunging into the fight, she asked Alice, "Why don't you know?"

"Because we haven't found Mother's will yet."

"For the last time, Alice—there wasn't any will!"

"Leon, you don't have to shout. We all heard you." She was again the controlled woman Joan remembered from Snarr's. "And Kitty says there was."

"Good God! Now you're going to believe Kitty! A minute ago you didn't trust her to put flowers in a vase."

"Excuse me," Joan said quietly. "I'm going to see how she's doing."

Nobody seemed to notice. The sounds of renewed quarreling followed her all the way down the hall. Guided by blue and white stenciling visible through a half-open door at the end of the hall, she found Kitty chopping onions at an old-fashioned kitchen table. Near the sink, the tulips and irises looked homey in a crock with a blue band.

"Can I help you with this?"

"No." Kitty scooped a mound from the chopping block into a bowl that matched the crock. "I better earn my keep." She wiped her eyes with the back of her hand and reached for another onion.

Joan took her at her word and pulled a chair up to the big old table. Not quite out of range of the onion fumes, but close enough to talk.

"Kitty, how long have you lived here?"

"Five years next month. Some days it feels like my whole life. But I'm glad. Mary Sue was the only other one who could've pulled up stakes and moved in like that, and she would've driven Edna crazy. I packed up my paints and came—there's an upstairs room with good north light."

"You were painting for a living?"

"That's what I told people. Actually, I was pretty desperate."

"Do you mind my asking—did Edna pay you?"

Kitty stopped chopping and shook her head. "She wouldn't have known how—never balanced a budget or a checkbook before her husband died. She was still in pretty good shape then, but not up to learning anything complicated. Later . . . well, you know about later. I had to stop painting then. There weren't enough hours in the day."

She lifted the hem of her apron to her eyes. Probably more than just onions. Joan felt a rush of sympathy.

"I'm so sorry."

"Mary Sue wrote the checks, such as they were. Edna never even knew. It wasn't much, but I had my room and board here, too."

"You took care of her—nursed her through to the end."

"She didn't need a nurse, not till the end. I just lived with her. I cooked for us both—her special diet and all— did the sugar tests, gave her the insulin, and did for this house what I'd do for my own." She looked around the big, comfortable room and her eyes filled up again.

"I did what I could—took her places, wrote letters for her while she still cared about hearing from people, shopped for her, stuff like that. Until she got so sick, she appreciated it—made me feel like family. Not like those two in there." She jerked her head in the direction of the living room and attacked another onion.

Not like Mary Sue, either, Joan thought, remembering the visiting hours at Snarr's. She stood, but hesitated to reach a hand in the direction of that blade.

"Edna was lucky to have you," she said. "So were her children. I hope they remember that."

WHEN SHE RETURNED to tell the others good-bye, the subject had changed and the mood had lightened. Alice and Leon were holding forth to Harold on family history. Joan wondered how long he'd been part of the family.

"We had brothers on both sides of the Civil War, you know," Alice said. "When Grandma was a little girl, Rachel Berry used to tell her stories."

"Like when she heard that Abner had been shot, only a few weeks after he married her," said Leon. "She took off to find him."

"That's right," said Alice. "She scoured the field hospital, but got nowhere. She was about to give up when they pointed her to the carts full of dead soldiers on their way to be buried."

"Young as she was, she was tough," Leon said. "She walked down the line of carts, looking at all those feet. She was looking for Abner's fine, handmade boots—she wasn't about to let them bury him with all the others."

He waited for Harold to respond.

"Why not?" Harold obliged.

"In those days the Berry name cut considerable ice in Kentucky. Grandma said Rachel considered herself lucky to have landed such a catch. She always called Abner 'Mr. Berry.' "

"Always?" And Harold chuckled.

"Harold!" Alice went prim again.

"Rachel never did find the boots," Leon said. "But she recognized Abner's bare feet sticking out of a pile of corpses. I don't know whether it was because of finding Abner or being mad about losing the boots, but the way Grandma told it, Rachel carried on loud enough to wake the dead. And I guess she did. The feet moved."

"They *what?*" Joan couldn't help it.

"They moved. Stacked like a piece of cordwood, Abner was still alive!"

"Half-dead is more like it," Alice said. "But Rachel took him home and nursed him back to health. They ended up with six or eight children. Kitty came down from them somehow—I'm not sure how."

Joan saw Harold repress a grin. We all know how, she thought, but he's not going to risk saying so. What kind of marriage must that be?

"Wasn't there something in the family about a Lincoln letter?" he asked instead. Joan could almost see the dol-

lar signs gleaming through his glasses. "Your mother used
to hint at it."

"She hinted at a lot of things," Leon said. "Mom
played her cards pretty close to her chest. You couldn't
take everything she told you as gospel."

"Leon!"

"Look, Alice, it's not what you'd call likely. After all,
old Abner was fighting on the wrong side. About his only
claim to fame back then was getting pulled out of that pile.
And they say later on he was a high muckety-muck in the
Klan."

"Leon! You don't have to tell everything!"

"Oh, loosen up, Alice. How long has Harold been in the
family? And I don't imagine we're shocking Joan with
ancient history."

A left-handed compliment, Joan thought, but I'll take
it. She shook hands all round and got out before they
started in on each other again.

SIXTEEN

Indiana Puzzle

ALL THURSDAY MORNING Fred had played phone tag with the coroner and Warren Altschuler.

At half past twelve he was biting into a ham on rye when the phone on his desk rang. Chewing, he picked it up left-handed.

"Lundquist," he said indistinctly.

It was Dr. Henshaw, with the autopsy results.

"I won't waste your time," he said. Fred translated: I won't waste my own. "Cause of death is blunt force. She had depressed fractures of the right parietal bone near the lambdoid suture."

"In plain English?"

"Multiple downward blows cracked the back of her head. Your old iron could have done the job, though we weren't able to match the fractures to it or see any pattern on the skin when we shaved the hair. It didn't break the skin, probably because her hair was so thick. There's no blood and virtually no hematoma—she died instantly."

"When?" Fred licked mustard off his right forefinger.

"Sometime between about ten Tuesday night and four Wednesday morning. That's based on rigor and body temperature in an unheated room. Tell me how late she last ate, and I can narrow it down from the remains of the ham on rye in her stomach."

Fred laid his sandwich on his desk—he knew better than to look at it just then. Leaning back, he stared at the ceiling.

"You said no blood. What about cuts?"

"They showed me those little scissors. But she didn't have a scratch on her. No defensive wounds. I did find some light facial contusions, though, consistent with falling forward after being hit on the back of the head."

"Forward?" Fred was sure Mary Sue had been flat on her back for hours by the time he saw her.

"I couldn't swear to it in court. But I think so, from the angle of the blows—and the marks on her face bear me out. If she'd bumped her face any earlier, you'd have seen them yourselves."

Had anyone noticed? Maybe even while she was still alive? Joan had seen her in the inn. So had the family. Fred leaned forward to scribble "marks" in his notebook, and then "last meal."

"Could the whole thing be an accident?" he asked. "Suppose she just fell and hit her head." Top-heavy as she was, he could easily see Mary Sue falling off one of those ladders.

"Then the fracture would extend up from below, not down from above. By the way, the blows were right-handed."

Great, Fred thought. That limits it to eighty-five percent of the population. But maybe less. Mary Sue was tall. With downward blows, he was looking for someone taller yet—or a short guy who brought along his own baseball bat.

"Besides," Dr. Henshaw was saying cheerfully, "you're going to have to account for that plastic. It doesn't look as if she asphyxiated—you can almost never be sure about that, but I didn't see any petechiae in the scalp or larynx—and she sure didn't pull up the covers."

"Yeah." Or put the ladders away. "What can you tell me about that?"

"From the postmortem lividity, someone rolled her over soon after death. All the discoloration was on the back. That's why the facial contusions were hard to spot."

"Anything else?"

"Only negatives. No bullets, no drugs, no poison, no disease, no sexual assault, no pregnancy."

FRED HAD FINALLY finished the sandwich and was fighting sleep in the old swivel chair when his office door creaked. His feet hit the floor and he jerked fully awake. Captain Altschuler's bulk filled the doorway.

"Relax." Warren Altschuler shut the door behind him and dropped heavily onto the wooden chair by the desk. "I got your message—and a call from the mayor. He's calmed down since last night. Seems his daughter overheard him chewing me out for not taking care of his baby. She gave him what for. Told him she was nobody's baby—old enough to make her own decisions, that sort of thing. Made him promise to apologize." He grinned. "Deckard's so button-busting proud of her, he gave it to me word for word."

Fred tried to imagine either of those big-eyed little girls intimidating the mayor. He shook his head and sat back down. "That's good news, anyway."

"Yeah. But he's thinking about not opening the show to the public until we clear up the homicide."

If we clear it up, Fred thought gloomily. Talk about cold trails. Deckard will think again when the economic implications of that little decision hit.

"We've let them go on setting up over there today," he said. "There was no point in sealing anything but that one room. People had been tramping through the rest of the inn all day yesterday, with her up there the whole time."

"You get time of death from Henshaw?"

"He says between about ten Tuesday night and four yesterday morning. The Elletts say she was alive after midnight."

"You believe them?"

"On that, yes. I'm not ready to think the whole family jumped her. But they may be hiding something. Leon stopped the women from answering my questions. Johnny Ketcham's over there trying again. He's got the best chance of getting through to them."

"Alone?"

"Yeah. They've known each other for years. Last night Alice welcomed him like a long-lost brother. If Leon isn't there to stop her and I'm not there to remind her who he is, I think she might open up to him."

"Could be. But don't stop there. Familiarity may make him accept something you'd question."

"Mmm." A new tune altogether from last year, Fred thought, when his superiors had considered him least likely to succeed.

"Just don't let the time slide by. What else?"

Fred filled him in on the rest of Dr. Henshaw's conclusions. Altschuler closed his eyes and shook his head.

"It's a damn shame they didn't find her sooner. Anything more from the scene?"

Fred pulled a report out of the rapidly growing file and passed it across the desk.

"Her keys are missing. They found her handbag with ID, charge cards, even cash—all there—covered by a quilt in a corner a few feet from her. But no keys."

"You check her house?"

Fred nodded. "Both the house and the car were unlocked. The guys who looked in said the house was so messy they couldn't guess whether anything was missing. We'll have to ask the family."

Flipping through the crime-scene report, Altschuler said, "I'll give you good odds there'll be more doors locked in Oliver tonight than there have been all last year. Some people live in the past."

Fred leaned back, feeling the wall behind his head.

"Trouble is, Mary Sue wasn't one of them. Oh, maybe at home—I don't really know. But not about the quilt show—and that's where she was. So where's her key to the Sagamore Inn?"

Digesting the implications, Altschuler groaned.

"You've posted someone at the door."

Fred nodded. "Deckard's little girl can sleep at home from now on." Sleep—he wished he could afford it. Forcing his feet back onto the floor, he stretched his cheeks around a close-mouthed yawn, but it got away from him. "I'm heading back over there to see what I can learn from the day people."

"Keep me posted." Altschuler got up.

Fred dragged himself out of the swivel chair and saw him out. Time to get moving. With Ketcham still at Edna Ellett's, he beckoned to Kyle Pruitt.

"Come on, Sergeant, let's go play detective."

THE MOOD AT THE INN was anything but playful. Not that Fred heard anyone mourning Mary Sue. The woman at the chair inside the door probably came closest. The pillowcases and bags that had hidden her two days ago had been replaced by papers.

"How was it here yesterday?" he asked her.

"Hectic," she said. "We had enough to do without this. Nobody could find her all day—well, now we know she was lying there dead, but I spent half the day thinking, just you wait till I get my hands on you, Mary Sue Ellett. I didn't know somebody already had, of course. I thought she'd skipped out at the busiest time, on the day of the judges' reception and all. It wasn't like her to leave us in the lurch like that, but it didn't occur to me that anything had happened to her, just that it was a major nuisance not to have her here. Now that we're having to decide things without her, we're finding out how much we depended on her good sense. She wasn't perfect—who is? But she knew how to run a show all right."

"How come nobody looked in that room?" Kyle waved toward it as if they could see through walls and ceiling to the yellow police barrier tape.

"Far as I know, the door was closed all day—not that I could see it. But even if somebody went in to look for her, they wouldn't have messed with a few quilts on the floor. We all had more than enough to do—that room was Mary Sue's problem. Well, her family's problem."

"There were quilts on the floor?" Fred asked softly.

"That's what I heard. Didn't you know?" She looked at him incredulously.

"I didn't," Kyle said, and it was true. "How did that happen?"

"Who had time to find out?" She waved her hands at the papers in front of her. "I told you, we were going crazy in here yesterday."

"Someone must have told you, then," Fred said. "Can you remember who?"

"Oh, everybody was talking about it when I came in this morning," she said. "I heard it first thing."

Great. It was the kind of detail only the killer might be expected to know, but already "everybody" was talking about it.

The killer—and Joan and Eddie, Fred reminded himself. Who'd spilled the beans? Personally, he'd put his money on Eddie, once the kid got past his first, shocked incoherence. One of the techs could have leaked it, but they were a well-disciplined lot. A far more likely possibility was that one of the white-gloved workers had looked into the room on Wednesday—maybe even entered it—and that now that she knew the significance of what she'd seen, she was afraid to come forward to the police but couldn't resist telling her friends.

"We'd better talk to those folks," he told the woman. "Who was here when you arrived?"

"Let me think. Mabel? No, Mabel came in later, with the judges. Esther? Could be Esther, I suppose, but I'm not sure just when she got here." She was starting to dither, but the dithering suddenly stopped on a practical note. "I don't see why you don't just ask one of your officers," she said. "They took our fingerprints before they let us in today."

"Thank you," Fred said. "We'll do that."

She looked relieved.

"If you're done with me, then..." Her voice trailed off.

"Unless you can think of anything that might help us."

"I can't imagine what. I mean, why would anybody want to kill Mary Sue?"

Resisting the temptation to remind her that she had spent the previous day wanting to do just that, Fred left her to whatever she was doing.

He set Pruitt to checking out the early arrivals.

"Don't get anybody's back up, Kyle," he warned. "Right now all we want to know is who got here early today and when the talk started. Let them bring up whatever they've heard.''

"You suspect one of them?''

"No. But it's possible. Come to think of it, check this lady's list of who was here Tuesday. It would have been easy for a worker to hang around late, after the doors were locked. From the sound of it, they all knew the Elletts were up there.'' The screech of electric saws echoed in his mind. "There should be men on that list, too—I saw carpenters here Tuesday.''

"Yessir.''

"Oh, and Kyle—I'll talk to Catherine myself.''

"Yessir.'' Kyle sounded relieved, and not without reason. The two redheads had struck sparks before.

It was a short walk from the inn to Catherine's Catering, a tiny kitchen that didn't hint at the quantity and quality of what she produced from it. As the jangling bell announced his presence, the pungent odors assailing Fred announced a wonderful stew. Catherine turned to welcome a potential customer. Her smile frosted over when she saw him.

"Slumming?''

"Catherine, I—''

"Don't you Catherine me. You haven't so much as called for months. You can't drop me flat for another woman and expect me to welcome you back when she doesn't have time for you anymore.''

She was getting a good running start—but on what, he didn't know. Burned first by his wife's infidelity and then by Catherine's jealousy over Joan Spencer last fall, he had indeed avoided her, but he'd steered clear of becoming involved with anyone else, including Joan. Damn, he thought. You've kept on controlling what I do, and I didn't even know I was letting you do it. That's going to stop right now.

He wiped all expression from his face, pulled his badge out of his breast pocket, and laid it on the showcase above the chocolate truffles.

"Police business."

That stopped her. She closed her mouth and wiped her fingers on her apron, carefully, one after the other. Finally she said, "I'm sorry, Fred. What's the matter?"

"I'm sure you've heard by now that Mary Sue Ellett's been killed. I can use your help."

"Fred, I don't know a thing about it. You can't think that I—" She seemed truly distressed.

"No, of course not. But you probably know more than you think." He tucked his badge back in his pocket and took out his notebook. "When did you see her last?"

"I—I don't really know." She was still flustered. He pressed her.

"When were you at the inn?"

"I've been there every day this week except Monday. The judges' reception . . ."

"Right. So think back. What was the last day you saw Mary Sue?"

"I saw her on Tuesday, I'm sure." She was avoiding his eyes now. "I couldn't tell you what time."

"Was it before or after you spoke to Joan Spencer?"

"What did she tell you?" Catherine was ready to attack again. He should have known.

"Don't worry about that. I've taken her statement. Now I'm interested in what you can tell me." Still, she hesitated. "Catherine, this is a homicide investigation. What's between me and Joan has nothing to do with it. And it is absolutely none of your business. Not now, and not ever again."

Her face crumpled. Damn. He was letting his personal affairs interfere with an investigation—exactly what he was accusing her of doing.

"I didn't mean..." A tear rolled down one cheek. Feeling heartless, but not taking it back, he handed her a clean white handkerchief. She dabbed at her mascara and blew her nose loudly.

"Thank you," she said in a muffled voice.

"You're welcome," he said, and waited until she had herself together again. When she looked up he asked softly, "So, what time did you see Mary Sue?" Her face was blotchy, but to his relief, she answered.

"I went upstairs and talked to her before I started working there. Sometime around four, I expect."

"Get paid?" Mary Sue would have signed her check, he knew.

"No. Well, I went back, but she was gone."

His antennae went out.

"How do you know?"

She responded with some of her old steam.

"For heaven's sake, Fred Lundquist, I called her name and she didn't answer. I figured I'd catch her the next day."

"And on Wednesday?"

"Same thing."

"You went into the room where the Elletts had been working?"

"No, I just opened the door and looked in. Nobody was there."

"What time was that?"

"Wednesday morning? Oh, about ten."

"How did it look?"

"I could see they hadn't finished. So I figured I'd try her at the reception. But I didn't see her there either."

He leaned on the case, careful not to put his weight on the glass. Having blown it once, he didn't want to distract her again from the business at hand.

"Think about what you saw in the room on Wednesday. Can you describe it?"

"Well, the walls looked done, but not all the quilts in the middle were hanging yet. There were a few on the floor—that surprised me, as fussy as quilt people are."

He let it pass without comment.

"Any ladders?"

"I didn't notice any."

He nodded and closed his notebook.

"Thanks, Catherine. That confirms what other witnesses have said. Oh, one more thing. Did you notice anything about her face when you saw her on Tuesday?"

"Her *face?*"

"Yeah."

"No."

"No bruises or anything?"

"No. She looked fine. A little heavy on the makeup for my taste, but nothing like what you're suggesting." Her nostrils flared then. She sniffed, grabbed a long wooden spoon, and took the lid off the stew. "Just in time," she said, stirring down to the bottom of the kettle. Fred's mouth watered.

"Thanks again," he said. "By the way, did you happen to mention any of this to anyone else?"

"Like what?"

"I don't know. Maybe the quilts on the floor?"

"Oh, that. Sure, I said something to one of those women with the white gloves. They act as if the mere smell of food would hurt their precious quilts, but I told them that the Elletts had theirs lying right on the floor." She looked at his face, and her own changed from satisfaction to horror. "Fred, she wasn't—I mean—Oh, no!"

"Thank you for your help, Catherine. I really appreciate it." And he dragged himself away, keeping it cool. Just in time, he thought. Another minute and I'd be tempted to say anything you want to hear, just to taste that stew.

SEVENTEEN

Silver and Gold

"HER WILL IS straightforward, Lieutenant," Mary Sue Ellett's young lawyer was telling Fred across a splendid mahogany desk in front of an impressive shelf of leather-bound volumes. His prematurely bald head gleamed above his bulging vest. "She made a couple of small bequests to charity. After that, she left everything evenly divided between her brother and her sister, with the understanding that they would care for their mother if she was still living."

"Which she wasn't." Fred leaned forward in the comfortable leather chair.

"No."

"Do you have an estimate of Mary Sue's estate?"

"No. I understand that there's some question about her mother's will."

"Assuming for the moment that she inherited nothing?"

The lawyer made a tent with his fingers and puckered his lips.

"Counting her house and her retirement plan, I'd estimate it in the vicinity of a hundred fifty thousand dollars."

Fred thought he could make moderate hay out of 150K, or even half that. It might not mean much to Alice and her CPA husband, but he was reasonably sure Leon would love nothing better than to lay his hands on that kind of money.

"Fairly liquid, would you say?"

"Not really. It will all have to go through probate, of course. But there was only a small savings account. The house will take a while to sell. Oliver's a slow market, and—well, frankly, the place will need some going over."

Shoveling out, Fred guessed, and grinned.

"The lady was quite a pack rat, wasn't she?"

The lawyer stiffened.

"I'm sure I didn't say that."

"No, you didn't need to." Fred smoothed his ruffled feathers. "And you haven't told me yet whether you drew up her mother's will."

"No, Mrs. Ellett never dealt with this firm."

"You don't know who did?"

"I can't help you there." The lawyer considered the ceiling. "You're not the first person to ask."

Fred wanted to strangle him for his professional coyness.

"Mary Sue, of course."

"No."

"Is her brother also your client? Or her sister?" Do I have to pull this out of you inch by inch?

"No."

"Did they ask about her will?"

"Mrs. Ellett's?"

"Yes." Fred gripped the arms of the chair and worked at not clenching his teeth. "Mrs. Ellett's."

"Only after my client's death. As per her previous instructions, I contacted them and notified them of the provisions of her will. They naturally asked about her estate, but I couldn't tell them any more than I could tell you."

"Only those two?"

"Oh, no." He moved a pencil an inch to the right, lining it up with the edge of his immaculate blotter. Give me patience, Fred thought.

"Suppose you tell me about all the rest."

"There was only one other, a Mrs. Graf." Kitty, the cousin. Of course.

"She was present when you read Mary Sue's will?"

"No. This was after Mrs. Ellett died." Fred felt his eyebrows shooting up. For once, the lawyer answered what he didn't ask. "That's right, Lieutenant. She was making inquiries about the old lady's will last week."

REBECCA MET JOAN AT the front door in cutoffs and bare feet.

"Your sleazeball boyfriend called."

"Rebecca!"

"I'm sorry, Mom." Rebecca shut the door and followed her into the living room. "I wasn't going to stick my nose in again. But I couldn't shut him up at first. And then I couldn't help leading him on. I'd been wondering just how much he'd admit to beyond kiting checks."

I suppose there are worse ways to find out what Leon's up to, Joan thought. Nudging her shoes off with her toes, she tossed her bag on the floor and flopped onto the old sofa, waiting.

Nothing.

Her eyes, which had closed as if she'd given them permission, opened again.

"So?"

"So you can't resist wanting to know, can you? Any more than I could."

"Okay, okay." Joan tossed a sofa pillow at her. It fell short. "What did you find out?" Rebecca grinned back from the safety of the overstuffed chair across the room.

"Enough to know I wouldn't trust him as far as I could throw him. He wants to take you out to dinner again and explain it all to you in person."

"I'll just bet he does. Rebecca, I don't think I could bear another minute with any member of that family."

"Maybe you should." Rebecca was suddenly serious. "I'll bet you'd learn a lot more from him than the cops will."

"They're going to have to do it without me. Honestly, Rebecca, I'm all in. Did Leon tell you anything at all, or just raise your hackles?"

"Oh, he told me, all right." Rebecca padded across the floor and perched on the arm at the far end of the sofa, facing her. "He's running a mortgage interest reduction service—at least, that's what he calls it."

"What do you mean?"

"It's a scam. You know, the kind of thing where someone offers to sell you money-saving tax tips for only nineteen ninety-nine, and when you pay, all you get is the 1040 instruction booklet?"

"People do that?"

"You'd be amazed. Leon's only a little subtler, but he'll make a lot more than nineteen ninety-nine a sucker."

"How do you know?" Joan sat up straight.

"It's one of the top-ten scams we hear about at the bank. Guys like Leon find out you're buying a house. They approach you, usually over the phone, with a great way to save you thousands of dollars on your mortgage payments. They'll make your payments for you twice a month instead of once a month, see, and all you have to do is pay them a monthly service fee—and one big payment up front."

"So it doesn't save me a thing?"

"Actually, it does. You save interest on the loan by paying half your payment early every month, and it mounts up fast. Even with the outrageous fees these guys charge, you do save thousands over the long haul, just the way they say."

"Then it's not a scam."

"It's not illegal, as long as Leon actually makes the payments. Just unethical. I mean, you could do it yourself without paying him a red cent, and save thousands more. Depending on the lender, you could probably pay twice monthly, the way he says he'll do. Or just add the fee you'd be paying Leon to your check every time you make a monthly payment. Or pay an extra monthly payment once a year or so."

"So it really is like buying something the IRS would send me free."

"Exactly. He never would have described it to me so beautifully if he'd known I worked in a bank. I think he was playing me both ways—as your daughter and as a possible home buyer. Once he found out I wasn't paying on a mortgage myself, he was more interested in telling you about it."

Joan laughed out loud and fell back against the cushions.

"I take it you didn't mention that Grandma and Grandpa Zimmerman left me this house free and clear."

"Did they?" Rebecca looked surprised. "Is that why you moved here?"

"It was a powerful inducement. What did you tell Leon?"

"Oh, I said I didn't know when you'd be home, and he said he'd try again around five."

"Thanks, Becca." She felt her eyelids drooping. "I should be asleep long before then. You wouldn't want to wake me." He sure fooled me, she thought. And then she didn't think at all.

THE SMELL OF curry filled her nose when she woke. In the darkening kitchen she found generous leftovers still warm enough to eat, and dug in. The curried rice tasted wonderful—she hadn't realized how hungry she was. Slowing down at last, she flicked on the table lamp and read a note: "Told Leon you were out like a light. Enjoy supper. R."

Leon. His name evoked a sadness that surprised her. It's not the first time I've been bamboozled, she thought. So why does it bother me so much? But she knew why. In spite of recognizing what Rebecca called his sleaze, she had been attracted to the big man. I didn't expect him to be honest, she told herself. But I didn't think he'd pull anything on *me*. Bamboozled is one thing. Betrayed is another.

She ran cold water over her plate and fork and tried to throw cold water on her emotions. Not only can I not trust Leon, I can't trust my own judgment.

Sure you can, a little voice inside told her. You never did trust Leon. You just didn't think he lied *all* the time.

Maybe he doesn't, she answered herself. But I thought I could tell when he would, and now I know I can't.

So how do I know he didn't kill Mary Sue? Could someone who doesn't quite break the law, but who doesn't mind cheating a woman he's attracted to, go from that to cold-blooded murder? Or *was* he attracted to me? Was that just as cold-blooded?

She shivered and turned off the water, leaving her plate to soak with the pot and the other dishes already in the sink.

Still, she thought, why would Leon pick the quilt show? He could get to Mary Sue anytime. Unless he was in a big hurry—what was it he said he needed money for? I wish

I'd listened better. I wonder whom Mary Sue left hers to. And how much she had to leave.

It felt like the middle of the night, but the curry had still been warm. Joan wasn't surprised when her digital clock radio displayed only eight o'clock. Lying on the bed, she dug in her handbag for Fred's card and dialed his home number.

"Yeah," he answered, sounding the way she had felt three hours earlier.

"Fred, it's Joan. Have you eaten?" Listen to me, she thought.

"If you could call it that."

"I can recommend what's left of Rebecca's curry. And I've learned something disturbing about Leon Ellett."

"Five minutes be too soon?"

She laughed.

"Not if you don't care what anything looks like."

"Hell, no."

Resisting the temptation to smooth the bedspread or check the state of the living room, she reheated the curry and brewed a pot of coffee. Then she set a kettle on the stove, too, in case he'd prefer tea with curry.

She answered the doorbell in stocking feet.

EIGHTEEN

Kitty Corner

SHE FED HIM FIRST. Sitting across the kitchen table, watching him savor the curry she, too, had found delicious, she was grateful again to Rebecca. Now, she thought, do I tell her she cooked supper for "my cop"? Probably not. But she told Fred.

"Thing is, if you'd asked me a week ago what Rebecca could cook, I wouldn't have known what to say after hot dogs. She left home so young, and not even faintly interested in anything so domestic."

He just nodded and held out his plate for seconds. Finally, she refilled their coffee, and they carried the mugs into the living room.

"So," he said from the big chair. "You had something to tell me about Leon Ellett?"

Joan, curled in the corner of the sofa, laid Leon's scam out to him as Rebecca had explained it to her, not exaggerating its wickedness, but wanting him to understand what it meant to her.

"Fred, he took me out. Rebecca would say he was coming on to me, but he was actually kind of sweet and shy and awkward. He *courted* me. So help me, it felt completely genuine. The old ladies saw through him, though. I should have believed them. He not only took me out—he took me in."

"At least you didn't lose anything," Fred said. "And he hasn't broken any laws."

She leaned forward urgently.

"No, but this changes what I told you about the Ellett family. At the funeral home Leon was Mr. Generosity, standing up against his mean sisters when it came to letting poor Kitty stay on in Edna's house. I don't know whether he put that act on for her benefit or mine, or maybe just out of habit, but I wouldn't give two cents for Kitty's chances now."

"You're probably right. Still, odds are that no one's going to own that house free and clear for quite some time. Looking good in the meantime is no skin off his nose."

"Right. But I can't help wondering . . ." She hesitated.

"What?"

"I don't know what Leon's mysterious land deals are all about, or whether they're real at all. But I do know he was really upset last week at not being able to get at his mother's money. And now, with Mary Sue out of the way, only Alice is likely to be standing between him and whatever Edna left all of them—unless maybe she left something to Kitty. What if Leon decided he needed more than his share?" You'd make a lousy poker player, she thought, watching Fred's eyebrows.

"You're serious." Now he was staring at her. She nodded.

"I know I'm mad at him, Fred. But I'm more than mad. I'm afraid he's dangerous." There. She'd said it. She felt her body relax.

"I'll keep him in mind," Fred said. "Leon was looking for Mrs. Ellett's will last week. But you'll be interested to know he wasn't the only one. Kitty Graf was asking lawyers about it."

"Kitty?" It hardly seemed likely. Kitty had been worried about survival, though, now that the family didn't need her to care for Edna. "Who told you that?"

"Mary Sue's lawyer. We're checking the other law firms, and the insurance agents, for that matter. You don't happen to know whether Edna was insured, do you? Or Mary Sue?"

"It never came up. But Edna must have had at least some insurance. For all their squabbling, no one was complaining about the expense of her funeral."

"Mmm-hmm."

"They didn't agree about a will, though. Seems to me at one point Leon said she didn't leave one at all, and Alice said she did. She said Kitty thought so. I don't know whether Kitty did, or that's just what Alice wanted me to hear. They made sure she was out of the room before they talked about it—at least it seemed that way. Someone else this week was certain she did leave one, though. I think someone at the center."

"What did Edna die of?" he asked suddenly.

"Flu, Alice said at Snarr's. Made worse by her diabetes. Kitty would know more—she was there."

"She the only one there?"

"Of the family? I think so. Why?"

"No witnesses?" He started to pace, swinging the empty mug between finger and thumb.

"How would I know? They must have had the doctor. Fred, what are you talking about?" She watched him, fascinated.

"It wouldn't be the first time someone was helped along a little."

"Ohhh." Why does the thought of Leon killing his mother bother me even more than thinking that he might have done in Mary Sue? "Leon?"

"Kitty, if she was the only one there." He walked faster. "She could have smothered her with a plastic bag—the carbon dioxide buildup would affect a diabetic fast. It crossed my mind when I saw Mary Sue under that plastic—until we rolled her over."

"Mary Sue was diabetic?" Joan was trying to catch up.

"Her body type was right for it—but that's not how she died. And this much later, I doubt that we'd ever be able to establish whether that's what did in her mother, even if we exhumed the body."

"Fred, that's outrageous!" It burst from her, and she jumped up. "Kitty wouldn't have killed Edna."

"Why not?"

"You should have seen them together. Besides, if you want cold, hard motives, killing Edna would have put her out of a job."

"And possibly gained her a house—without the trouble of working to keep it. Though, if you're right about Leon, Mary Sue wasn't the only one who stood in her way. I don't know how she would have planned to get rid of Alice."

"But to kill for it?" Joan was toe to toe with him now, and too mad to enjoy it. "Fred, you're way off. You didn't see her after Edna died. She was devastated."

"All right, you've convinced me," Fred said, dropping it abruptly and staring her down. "Try this, then. She didn't plan to kill anyone—she went at those quilts with scissors, in revenge against the whole family. And Mary Sue caught her at it."

"That's the first sensible thing you've said." She sank back onto the sofa. "But Leon still fits a lot better than Kitty. Only it wouldn't have been for revenge. They were all hunting for Edna's will. They probably figured she lost it, but maybe she hid it, instead. She was more than forgetful—she was losing charge of her own life. She had to have known it. She may have wanted to be sure that her children wouldn't destroy her will. Leon would have, for sure, unless it left him more than his fair share. And what better place to hide a piece of paper than inside a quilt? Did I tell you about the note she tucked into the orchestra quilt?''

"Paper," Fred said thoughtfully. "As in paper money."

"Better yet. Leon was in such a hurry for cash. Wouldn't he love to find it where he could just walk off with it! No probate, nothing to slow him down." Even old Mrs. Brown from the center had emptied a joint account and lockbox before the bank found out her husband was dead—because, she'd told Joan afterwards, she couldn't bear to wait months for what was rightfully hers.

"We're looking into the cuts in those quilts. We've taken all the ones that were cut into over to the station. If there's anything in them, we'll find it."

"You won't wreck them, will you, Fred? I hear some of them are old and special. They say Edna never showed them."

"Don't worry, we'll be careful. We won't have to do much— Kitty really opened them for us."

He's still sure it's Kitty, Joan thought, feeling a rush of sympathy for the woman.

"I don't believe it," she said firmly. "For one thing, how could she? Kitty's too little to cut those quilts down standing on the floor, and the ladders are gone."

"We don't know when the ladders were moved."

"True, but Leon wouldn't even have needed a ladder. Why are you stretching, Fred, when the obvious answer is staring you in the face?"

He finally stopped pacing and balanced the mug on a stack of Andrew's textbooks.

"I've been holding out on you, Joan. We found a couple of hairs."

"Can you establish identity from a couple of hairs?"
Joan thought it unlikely.

"Not unless there's enough root tissue and skin cells attached for a DNA match, and we don't have that. But we
can narrow it down from what we do have. Alice's hair is
long and straight, Mary Sue bleached hers, and Leon's
going gray. At first glance, Kitty's the only one of the
family they could have come from. We'll match them with
her hairbrush—the search warrant should have arrived by
now."

"What about Harold? He doesn't have much hair, but
what he has looks a lot like Kitty's. Leon said Alice could
pretend all she cared about was family, because she knew
Harold would see to it that she got hers. Not that I believe
anything Leon says, but he sounded bitter enough that he
may not have been putting that on. And Margaret Duffy
said at the center the other day that Harold and Alice had
made a bad cross-country move and couldn't afford to
change their minds and come home."

Fred nodded and scribbled something in his notebook.
"Thanks. We'll check it out."

"And how about prints? Weren't there fingerprints on
the plastic?"

"Smudges, most of them. Useless. Too many people
had handled it. There were some lipstick smudges on it,
too, and one clear print of Mary Sue's lips—too bad that's
no help."

Joan shuddered to think of circumstances in which a
victim's lip prints might help. It was a use she had never
thought of for Mary Sue's heavy makeup. She refused to
be side-tracked.

"I don't know how those hairs got there, Fred Lundquist, or whether they came from Kitty. But they don't
prove a thing and you know it. Even if you establish that

they were hers, all you'll know is that she was there. We already know she was there. So were all the rest of them— I saw them myself. For that matter, maybe someone else took them out of her hairbrush and planted them at the scene.''

"I'd hate to come up against you in court." He sat down beside her. "You're right, of course. That kind of circumstantial evidence would never hold up. I can't make a case—yet. But I'll keep digging.''

"That's what I'm afraid of.''

"The truth?'' He was smiling down into her eyes now.

"I don't know. I don't think so.'' She wasn't sure just what she was afraid of. I can trust this man, she told herself. He's not Leon. But how can he be so pigheaded? Doesn't he know he can hurt an innocent person?

Then the back door slammed, and she jumped like a guilty teenager.

"Mom? Rebecca?'' It was Andrew.

"In the living room,'' Joan called back. She grinned up at Fred. "Come see who's here.''

Fred met Andrew halfway across the room.

"I was just leaving. You tell your sister she makes a mean curry.''

"She said she was going to leave me some. You ate it, huh?'' Andrew slid Fred's mug off his books onto the end table and started rummaging in the pile. "It's probably just as well. I'm a ham-and-eggs man myself.''

The tension broke, Joan padded to the door with Fred. She'd see him at the Sagamore Inn on Saturday, when the orchestra would make one last stab at a dress rehearsal.

After he'd left, it was all she could do not to warn Kitty.

NINETEEN

Spring Beauty

"NOPE. ASK MOM—or walk."

"Andrew, come on! It's a long way out there."

"Sorry, Bec. I need it. See you." The back door slammed.

Standing at her bedroom window, Joan looked down. Hunched over his low-slung handlebars, Andrew was already pedaling toward school. She breathed in April freshness. Moist leaves and soil warming in the sunshine.

You can almost smell the worms, she thought—and the mushrooms. At home I'd know where to hunt.

Home. It took her by surprise every time. Would she never feel that Oliver was home?

Now she heard Rebecca climbing the stairs. She girded herself to say no.

I don't want to be without the car, any more than Andrew wanted to lend his bike. But it won't be easy for me— I know what she'll say.

She said it.

"You always walk to work, Mom. Mind if I borrow your car for the morning?"

"Where do you want to take it?" Even old private Rebecca would have to admit that that was her business.

"Just out to Carolyn Ryrie's cabin. She's dyeing today. She says she'll show me the whole process."

"Oh? Where's the cabin?" Joan was stalling, and knew it.

"Off old 46, in woods near the state forest. She drew me a map."

The curtains flapped, giving Joan another overwhelming whiff of spring. Why not? she thought. I could play hooky in the woods. While they're dyeing, I'll commune with nature. I'll love it. And I deserve it.

"Rebecca, I'll be happy to take you out," she said. "Hang on while I make a phone call." Turning her back on any objections Rebecca might raise to having her mother along, she started dialing.

"I'll be back this afternoon," she told the center. "I'm not sure when."

Already dressed for work, she changed to a long-sleeved flannel shirt, jeans, socks, and her oldest sneakers. She stuck a wad of toilet paper in one pants pocket, just in case, and went down to the kitchen for a couple of wax-paper bags, which she tucked into her other pocket. She'd soon forget them if she didn't need them. But far more frustrating than finding no mushrooms would be finding more than she could carry.

It was a short drive, but beautiful.

Near the edge of town, the blacktop gave way first to gravel and then to dirt. Huge weathered woodpiles and bales of uneaten hay suggested that the locals had been prepared for much worse than the mild winter Joan had appreciated after long years in Michigan.

They rode in silence past splotchy grass, with wild onions already green and tall. Here and there the sun glinted off the windshields of abandoned cars and trucks, their bodies dull with rust. Dried cattails waved stiffly in a ditch on one side of the road; on the other, raspberry canes stretched new red tips toward the earth.

Along the curve of a little creek, sycamores with last year's balls hanging from their bare branches stood out white against a newly plowed field. A haze of green interrupted by delicate red-brown patches and occasional dark green pines marked the beginning of the woods ahead.

At a fork where dead-looking branches crossed the road above them, Rebecca came to life.

"This is it." She held out the map Carolyn had drawn the day they worked on the orchestra quilt. "You turn up that way. Then left at the little bridge. That's the Oliver reservoir."

The road narrowed to a one-lane track surrounded by increasingly dense woods. They came to a clearing.

"There's her car," said Rebecca.

"It *is* a cabin!" Joan had pictured a small house, not these roughhewn logs. She pulled up and they both got out. Any minute now she expected Abe Lincoln to stride through the doorway. "Do you think it's genuine?"

Coming around the cabin, Carolyn answered her. "Only the front room. The rest has been added piecemeal. Come on in—I'll show you."

Joan hesitated. Driving Rebecca out was one thing, but horning in on her visit would be another.

"Oh, come on, Mom. You know you're itching to see it." True.

"I'd love to, but I won't stay. I came to walk in the woods."

"This won't take long." Carolyn ducked into the low doorway. Walking through straight up, Joan felt the frame brush the top of her hair. Abe never would have made it.

A fieldstone fireplace and hearth dominated the dim room, and a ladder led to a dark loft. While Rebecca oohed and aahed, Joan wondered how many people had once lived in this small shelter. She tried to imagine winter months with small children.

"How did they see to quilt?" Rebecca marveled.

"Not very well, even in the daytime," said Carolyn. "I wouldn't try." And she led them through the kitchen and past a bedroom and bath to her workroom, clearly a recent addition, with large windows on three sides and a skylight directly over a large table. Open cubbyholes on the long inside wall held folded pieces of fabric—blues here, reds there, yellows and browns farther along. Drawings on translucent paper lay on the table. At one end of the room stood an empty quilting frame, its poles wrapped in white cloth.

Carolyn showed off lights recessed in the white ceiling. "I had them put in. Now day and night are the same to me."

"What a great studio!" Rebecca was poking her nose into corners. "I'm getting ideas already." She looked at the drawings on the table. "Your designs are beautiful. Are they for a new one?"

"No, this is the one they stole." Carolyn slid the drawings into one of many wide, shallow drawers built into the table. "Let's go back outside. I need to check the fire."

"You dye outside?" Joan asked.

"Sure. Spills don't matter out there, and I don't have to worry about fumes."

Time for me to take off, Joan thought, and did. She left the two of them huddling like the witches in *Macbeth* and muttering about mordants.

A narrow path led into the woods but soon disappeared. Looking back for landmarks, Joan took her bearings from the sun and the long shadows cast by the trees. It was old forest, with little underbrush—once the mature trees leafed out, few saplings would have a chance at sunlight. Her eyes followed the tall, straight trunks of oaks and tulip poplars up to their crowns until she felt dizzy. Then she sat down, leaned her head back against a beech, and listened to the silence. Only the soft rustle of the tree-tops far above her proved that she could hear at all.

Gradually, although she couldn't see them, she began to hear birds. Then, in the distance, she heard a hollow hammering. Sounds like a big one, she thought, and watched. The hammering came again, and the unmistakable silhouette of a pileated woodpecker appeared on a tree across a deep gorge—Woody in the feathers. She wondered how her tree would sound if the bird attacked while her head was still touching it, but it kept its distance. Then she stood up, stretched, and looked for a stick to poke the dead leaves.

A couple of hours later she hadn't found a single mushroom, but she'd hiked hillsides covered with bloodroot and cut-leaf toothwort in full bloom, budding trillium and fuzzy wild poppies, and May apples with their leaves furled. It was too soon to see jack-in-the-pulpits or fiddleheads—only the Christmas ferns were green—but the spring beauties were out, and the trout lilies were the biggest she'd ever seen.

Her calves aching from climbing the steep hills, Joan felt at peace. She turned back toward the cabin, aiming for the sun, and was delighted to arrive, if not at the path she had taken behind it, then at least in the clearing in front of it.

An old red pickup had joined the cars, and she could hear a man's voice coming from behind the cabin.

"You know I'm good for the money. When did I ever let you down?" he pleaded softly in the accents of rural southern Indiana. His voice sounded vaguely familiar.

Joan walked around the cabin. Now she could see him. A tall man, he bent as if he were trying to hide his chest. The wiry arms sticking out of his shirtsleeves sprouted hair as sandy as the wisps sticking out through the back of his ventilated John Deere cap. When he turned and she saw his face, she recognized him as the man who had delivered Snarr's folding chairs to the inn. His full attention was fixed on Carolyn.

Carolyn snorted.

"Let me down? You don't call taking off without a word letting me down? I was worried sick—I kept imagining you lying in a ditch and no one coming to help. But then someone saw you in Martinsville. That was weeks ago. You didn't so much as call until today."

"A man's got to have his freedom."

"Not at my expense." Carolyn turned her back on him and stirred a dye pot with a stick. Briefly, Joan's eyes met Rebecca's. They kept their faces still.

"I told you, I'll pay you as soon as I get back. When this deal goes through, we'll be in clover."

"There's no way you could..." Carolyn's voice trailed off. She turned to face him. "Actually, Ralph, there is something. And it won't cost you a thing."

"Uh-huh." He wasn't having any.

"I mean it. You still have that last shirt I made you?"

His jaw tensed. "Why?"

"You put that up as collateral, and I'll lend you the money."

"Now why would you do a thing like that?"

"I'm having trouble matching the browns."

"It's pretty beat up. Got a big hole in it."

Carolyn didn't flinch. "I don't care. I don't need the shirt, just the fabric. And only for a few days. You can have it back—if you want it."

"You really mean it."

"I mean it."

"I won't say no. And hey, I'm sorry."

"It's all right, Ralph." She flashed him a smile Joan thought could melt a man down into a puddle. "Any chance you'd go after it today, while we're still working here?'' She waved her stick at the fire.

Uh-huh, Joan thought. Maybe he was going to get a loan, but if he thought he was going to pick up with Carolyn where he left off, he was in for a surprise. This was business.

"Sure thing. I'll be right back." Acknowledging Joan and Rebecca for the first time with a two-fingered salute that almost made it to the bill of his cap, he started for his truck.

Then Rebecca spoke quietly into Carolyn's ear. She nodded.

"One more thing, Ralph," she said. He pulled up short. There was going to be a catch to it, after all.

"When you come back, could you give Rebecca a lift into town?"

Rebecca beamed at Joan.

"We're just getting a good start, Mom. There's no reason you should hang around, if Ralph will take me home." Translate that as hang around and cramp my style, Joan thought.

"Glad to." Visibly relieved, Ralph swung into the pickup and raised a cloud of dust down the road toward town.

Joan had a sinking feeling about entrusting Rebecca to him. But I'm not, she told herself. Rebecca's doing the entrusting. Why is that so clear when she's far away and so foggy when we're standing next to each other?

"I'm sorry you had to hear all that," Carolyn told her. "I would have sent him packing if it weren't for that shirt."

"The one you were talking about the other day? That matches your stolen quilt?''

"That's it. Ralph doesn't need to know I'm going to display it in public—I hope it's not too far gone. Sometimes he's hard on clothes."

"Doing what?" Rebecca asked. Joan wondered how hard embalming people was on clothes.

"Just about everything. He can fix anything from a car to a computer, and does. He did a lot of the work on my cabin and taught me how to stack wood and clean a chimney. You need skills to survive the simple life in the nineties, and Ralph's a surviver. But I know better now than to count on him."

Joan wished her good luck, told Rebecca she'd see her when she saw her, and left for home.

Less than half an hour later, without exactly having decided to stop, she was sitting in Fred's office telling him about it. "It's probably nothing," she said. Rebecca would call that discounting herself.

"'Probably nothing' is where some of our best leads come from. Think I'll call Sergeant Pruitt in on this one." He picked up the phone.

Joan remembered the solid man with freckles who appeared at the office door.

"C'mon in, Kyle," Fred said. "You've met Mrs. Spencer."

"Yes, sir. Ma'am."

Joan repeated her brief story. Pruitt blushed when she came to Carolyn's obvious anger. She didn't try to guess why, but went on to describe the deal Carolyn had struck.

"So he's going back to take her a brown shirt—about now, if he meant what he said."

Pruitt sat up even straighter, if that was possible.

"Brown? Cotton? Printed like her quilt?" He seemed to know all about Carolyn's quilt.

Joan nodded.

"What does this Ralph look like?"

"Kind of a tall, skinny version of you. Maybe thirty-five."

Fred chuckled at that, and Pruitt blushed again, but he didn't quit.

"I don't suppose you saw him run?"

"Run?" Puzzled, she shook her head. "He just walked over to his pickup and climbed in."

"How was he dressed?"

"Red-and-black-checked shirt and blue jeans. Boots. A John Deere cap." Pruitt was nodding.

"Worth checking out, don't you think?" Now he was asking Fred. Joan was completely lost.

"Is there something I ought to know? My daughter's planning to ride home with this character."

TWENTY

Catch Me If You Can

KYLE PRUITT'S round face lost its smugness.

"Call it off," he urged.

Fred drew a blank.

"You going to clue me in?" he asked. And then it hit him. "You think . . . ?"

"I sure do," Pruitt said. "Last week, when the lady was describing her stolen quilt, I thought something sounded familiar. So I took a look at those scraps in the evidence bag—the ones they picked off the fence after the guy got away that night. Sure enough, one good-sized brown hunk had black lines near the edge, a lot like what she was telling me about. For a minute there, I thought maybe it wasn't a guy, after all—maybe they took her for a man. She's plenty tall. But they wouldn't miss those boobs." He blushed. "Pardon me, ma'am."

Joan rolled her eyes. Fred suspected she'd heard worse.

"Just give me a phone book." Her words came out shaky.

Fred pulled rank on the information operator instead, but didn't find so much as an unlisted number for Carolyn Ryrie. We'll have to head him off, he thought.

"What's this Ralph driving?" he asked Joan.

"An old Ford pickup."

"Color?"

"Red, but I think he's painted it. It's too dull to be original."

He gave her time to see it again. "What else?"

"He's got one of those scenes on the back window of the cab. A lake, with mountains." She gulped and avoided his eyes. "The sun was behind me. I couldn't see through it." To the gun rack, he thought. She was hanging tough.

"What about the truck bed? Could you see what he was carrying?"

"There was stuff back there. A couple of tires. Ladders. I think maybe some gravel. No tailgate."

"Did you see the plate?" Not likely.

"Not really. I wasn't trying. It didn't look like Indiana, though."

"Oh?"

"It was plain white, and there wasn't any letter after the first two numbers." Just a truck license.

Her control slipped then, and she grabbed his arm. "Fred, don't let him hurt her!" He covered her hand with his and turned to Pruitt.

"Kyle, have someone pick up Carolyn Ryrie and bring her here with that shirt. You won't need a warrant—she'll cooperate. First, though, put out a call to locate Ralph." It was too much to hope that Joan would know Ralph's last name, but he asked.

She didn't. "But you could ask Snarr's. Ralph's the man they sent over to the inn with the chairs. You've seen him, Fred. Remember?"

He nodded. "Check with Snarr's. Sergeant. You've got his description. Be sure you put the word out that if he's spotted on the way back to town, he'll have Rebecca Spencer with him."

He had to ask Joan. "What does she look like?"

"Like Andrew, only my height and a girl. Short hair and all. She's wearing jeans and a blue T-shirt." She had herself back under control now.

"White female, age twenty, five-five, slender build, fair complexion, short dark curly hair."

Joan nodded.

"Add the clothes and what you heard about the vehicle. He's wanted for questioning, could be armed. Just have him followed—no confrontation as long as she's in there—we don't want this to turn into a hostage situation. He might be headed for Snarr's, but it's a good guess he'll drop her off at Chestnut and Prospect."

"Let's hope we get to him before he picks her up in the first place."

"Don't spook him trying. We don't have a thing on him—yet."

Pruitt took off and Fred turned to Joan.

"I'm afraid your job will be harder."

She sat very still.

"He's seen your car?"

A nod.

"So you'd better look normal. Go home, go to work, whatever. And try not to worry. If we're wrong about this guy, there's no problem. Even if we're right, she's probably safe enough as long as nothing tips him off. Last time, he ran. He might not know what a good description we got of him that night."

"What did he do?"

"If we're right? He stole the hard drives out of half the computers at Oliver College, and some extra chips and cards besides."

"Computers?" Some of the tension left her voice and face.

That's right, Fred thought, reading her. Just things.

"It's turned the campus upside down, and the businesses are getting nervous. People all over town are carrying their micros home at night."

"Why do you think it's Ralph?" she asked.

"You heard Sergeant Pruitt. Your description fits the man we almost caught in the act. Mostly he blends into the woodwork, but that night he snagged his clothes on a fence. If the pieces in our evidence bag match Ralph's shirt, we'll know he's our man. And this time we've got surprise on our side."

She was leaning forward now, the spark back in her eyes.

"Fred, Ralph said it had a hole in it!"

Better and better. Then the spark died, and her forehead creased.

"Oh, Fred. Oh, no. How could I forget?"

"What?"

"Ralph was at the inn before Mary Sue died. He was looking around and kind of joking about what a firetrap it was and how they were probably insured against loss."

"Uh-huh." Probably considering a hit.

"Then he got to talking about Mary Sue."

Now Fred leaned forward.

"And?"

"She owed him money. He was mad about it. And he embalmed her mother at Snarr's. Fred, maybe *Ralph* killed Mary Sue. It would be natural as breathing for him to lay her out like that. And now Rebecca's riding with him." She shuddered.

He looked her over. Her color was all right.

"We'll get him. You going to be okay?"

"I'll fake it. I'm going home. No one's expecting me back at work yet anyhow, and I'll do better alone."

"You sure?"

"I'm tougher than I look." The shakiness was gone. "But you take care of Rebecca."

He walked her to the door. She didn't look back.

WITH HOURS OF paperwork piled in front of him, Fred was doodling trucks on his blotter. Nothing yet from Snarr's— the answering service had said they were all at an interment in a little country cemetery near Gnaw Bone, but did he need a body picked up? Finally, Kyle Pruitt stuck his head in.

"A sheriff's deputy spotted them coming into town. The girl's with him. She looked okay, and he wasn't acting nervous or anything."

"Where?"

"Turning right off Bottom Road onto Fox Hollow. They'll be on Main in another couple of minutes."

Fred stood up and reached for his jacket.

"Let's go."

Kyle wanted to use the siren; Fred could see it in his eyes. But he had more sense. Instead, they took back streets and occasional alleys, listening to the radio dispatcher track the pickup.

Near campus they passed under power lines hung with pairs of sneakers dangling by their strings. No matter when the electric company plucked them, a new crop of the strange fruit always sprouted within days. Fred had sometimes suspected ritual significance. A before-exam safety ritual? A before-sex safety ritual? Or maybe just celebrations, as people said—an enterprising student could always think of something to celebrate.

Today he hardly noticed them.

The radio spoke.

"Now entering S-curve; downtown units stand by."

"Let's pick him up at Main."

Kyle obliged with a sharp swerve. "There he is."

"Yeah, I see him." *Or would, if I could see through the back window of the cab.* "Hang back until he drops her off."

Sedately, they followed the dull red pickup through downtown, separated now by one car, now by two. So far, so good. The truck was less than a block north of Prospect when some fool in a unit coming up behind them hit his siren.

"What the—!" Fred grabbed the radio, but it was already too late. The pickup made a screeching U-turn, giving him a look at its occupants—the grim-faced driver spinning the steering wheel, and the girl, her mouth open wide and her hand clutching the roof.

Kyle's foot hit the brakes. His eyes begged Fred.

"Go ahead. It can't hurt now." Sliding down into the seat, Fred braced his feet against the floorboards. Kyle slapped the flasher onto the roof, cut loose with the siren, and followed on two wheels. The pickup led them back through town toward the campus. Fred filled the dispatcher in as they went.

The sneakers flew by overhead. Then they were careening around the Oliver College admissions office into the arboretum on a road marked "Service Drive Only." Between trees, Fred caught glimpses of red.

"We've got him!" Kyle exulted. "This one dead-ends at the library."

"Don't count on it. He's not about to sit there and wait for us."

Running wasn't one of Kyle Pruitt's strong points, and the officers who had lost this guy before could outrun either of them. But Fred had planned ahead.

"Campus backup needed at the library—he's coming in at the loading dock," he told the dispatcher.

"Ten-four."

The library loomed ahead.

To Kyle's credit, he pulled up when the driver's side door of the pickup swung open. Rolling out and landing on his

feet, Fred shouted, "Police! Freeze! Hold it right there!"
But Ralph, crouching, had already put the truck between
them and was dodging through the trees behind the library. Fred couldn't see a weapon.

Kyle gave chase; Fred looked into the cab of the pickup.
Pale, but apparently uninjured, Rebecca looked so much
like her brother that he thought he would have recognized
her cold. At a glance he took in the torn upholstery, the
overflowing ashtray, the soiled floor littered with cans and
flip-top tabs, and the decrepit gray blanket covering who
knew what in the space behind the seat.

The gun rack was empty.

"Police," he said, showing Rebecca his badge through
the open window on the driver's side. "You all right?"

"Yes, but—"

"Is he armed?"

"Armed! With what?" Good. She couldn't have missed
much of anything under Ralph's jeans. Fred relaxed a little.

A police car pulled up behind them. Glad to see two
speedy young officers, he pointed them in the general direction of Ralph's flight.

"What's going on?" Rebecca had slid down out of the
pickup and was staring at him warily from the passenger
side.

"Did this man just take a brown shirt out to Carolyn
Ryrie's?"

"How did you—?" He watched her face work its way
from startled through curiosity and around to indignation. "What is this, anyway? What business is it of the
police?"

"He's suspected of grand larceny." No point in worrying her with more than that.

"You think he stole Carolyn's quilt!" There was a thought.

"No," he said. "We're chasing down some missing equipment."

"Chase him, then—all I did was bum a ride." Now she was on the defensive.

Unlikely as Joan's daughter in cahoots with a local thief seemed, caution died hard.

"I leave chasing to faster people. And I don't want him to circle back and drive this heap off again." Or you, he added silently.

"Don't worry." He saw Joan in her dancing eyes. "He can't."

"How's that?"

"That was some ride, once he heard the siren. He left his keys in the ignition when he took off. I threw them over there in the bushes."

"And to think that your mother worried about you."

She looked blank for just a moment, and then her face lit up.

"You're Mom's cop!"

He could hear Andrew saying it.

She stuck out her hand. "Rebecca Spencer—but you already know that, don't you?"

"Fred Lundquist." They shook hands across the hood. Hers was firm and warm—she'd already recovered.

"She told you about Ralph."

He nodded. "A little. What's his last name?"

"I never did hear. Carolyn must know. She wrote him a check when he arrived with the shirt. And she made him sign a note."

Joan hadn't mentioned money.

"He was strapped?" You'd think he'd have cashed in some of his chips, so to speak. Maybe Ralph wasn't the computer thief, after all.

"I guess. He said he needed money for a trip. He promised Carolyn he'd pay her as soon as he got back."

That figured. All the publicity would make it next to impossible to sell stolen computer chips anywhere near Oliver. Time to check Ralph's ID and notify the banks.

A second car arrived. He sent one man after Ralph and asked the other, a lanky recruit named Wampler, to stay — both in case the fox doubled back and to witness his search for the truck's registration.

With Rebecca watching too—another witness, Fred thought comfortably—he climbed into the cab and started with the glove compartment. After pencil stubs, cigarettes, small change, matchbooks, old lottery tickets, and a penlight, he came to a grubby owner's manual held together by rubber bands. A likely place for the registration. He pulled it out—and rejoiced.

"Will you look at that," said Wampler, who was tall enough to stare over Fred's shoulder into the glove box at the clear plastic bags the manual had concealed. "Drugs?"

"Computers. Probably hard drives." Compact and ready to drive to market. For all his own mess, Ralph apparently knew enough to keep them clean. "We're going to make some people very happy today." Starting with me, Fred thought. "Let's find out who he is."

Leaving the bags where they were, he climbed out of the pickup, pulled the registration out of the rubber bands, and laid it on the hood. The truck was registered to a Ralph Lloyd Wampler. Oliver had about as many Wamplers as Deckards.

"Ralph Lloyd?" The recruit was standing almost at attention. "I've never heard of him, sir."

"We won't hold him against you, Wampler." Fred laid his hand on the young man's shoulder. "Go call it in—if he gets away, he might try to cash that check locally. And get us a warrant to search the rest of this truck."

"Yes, sir." Wampler loped back to his unit. Rebecca seemed to have disappeared. Fred scanned the woods. No Rebecca. Oh, God. I can't lose her now.

"Look!" He whirled at her triumphant shout. "See what I found!" She had dragged the old blanket down onto last year's leaves. Now she nudged it with her toe. Unrolling before their eyes, it revealed a puffy brown lining, with intricate designs of ferns, stalks, leaves, and fungi printed in black against a subtly pieced background, shaded from dark walnut at the bottom to a few pale inches at the top. Vertical strips and closely spaced lines of quilting effectively suggested tree trunks.

Carolyn Ryrie's quilt, without a doubt. Fred had no idea whether it had a shot at the prize, but he could see why she might expect it to.

They were going to make a few more people happy, he thought. Not only had Ms. Ryrie's missing property been found, but finding it in Ralph's truck pretty much wiped out any connection to the quilt show. From what Joan had said, it might be part of a lovers' quarrel. He looked forward to giving Captain Altschuler the good news. Too bad he couldn't tell Mary Sue.

"Congratulations," he told Rebecca instead. "How did you know?"

"I didn't," she said. "When Ralph peeled rubber back on Main Street, something that felt like a sleeping bag saved me from whiplash. It made sense—he was leaving town. I didn't tumble to it until the door was open and I was standing on the ground here, looking in behind you.

That's when I saw brown in the end of his blanket roll.''
Her eyes sparkled. "I had to be sure.''

"We would have found it, you know. I can't say I'm
sorry that you did, but I have to ask you not to touch anything else. I've sent Officer Wampler for a search warrant.'' He didn't want her to plunge into the truck again,
this time under what might be construed as his influence.
There was no hurry now, and it would be a shame to lose
old Ralph Lloyd and whatever else might have been hidden under that blanket over some nitpicker's interpreta-
tion of legal search. But Rebecca seemed to have lost
interest in the pickup. She was staring past him.

"We got him, Lieutenant.'' The voice in his ear startled
Fred. Officer Root had pulled up soundlessly on one of the
new police bicycles, her radio antenna sticking up above
her shoulder.

"It worked?''

"Like a charm. He ran from the guys crashing through
the brush, and we surprised him on the sidewalk. They're
bringing him back now.''

So they were. Fred watched the awkward parade down
the little slope toward them. Held firmly by each arm and
handcuffed behind his back, Ralph stumbled occasionally over the rough spots. Two more bicycle cops brought
up the rear.

"Peter and the Wolf,'' Rebecca said.

TWENTY-ONE

Best of All

TRYING NOT TO watch at the window, Joan missed seeing Fred's Chevy pull up. But she heard Andrew whoop and raced him to the door.

Now there was no need to hold back. Rebecca ran straight into her embrace, and Joan's eyes met Fred's beyond her daughter's curly head.

"How can I ever thank you?"

"Rebecca's already taken care of that." He beamed at both of them. "First she immobilized his vehicle and then she found the missing quilt."

Rebecca needed no urging to tell the whole story. When she finally ran down, Joan asked, "Where's Ralph now?"

"Over at the station being booked," Fred answered. "What we found in the glove compartment was the tip of the iceberg. Most of the rest of the missing computer parts were hidden under the quilt. I've sent a man out to bring Ms. Ryrie back with the shirt."

Relieved as she was, Joan found herself feeling almost sorry for Ralph. To him, Carolyn's creation was probably just a bedcover, she thought, and said so.

"Don't you believe it," Fred said. "You're forgetting about the piece of his shirt in our evidence bag. It doesn't matter, now that we've got him dead to rights with the stolen goods. But before that, he didn't want any public display of a design that could lead us to him."

"So he stole the quilt that matched his shirt." Joan shook her head. "And then Carolyn talked him into lending her the shirt back by telling him she wanted to match the browns. He never would have taken it to her if he'd known she was planning to display it at the show!"

"I wonder if they'll let her enter her quilt now," Rebecca said.

"That's the kind of decision Mary Sue Ellett would have made," said Fred. "I don't know how flexible the rest of them are. It's in our evidence room, of course, but we ought to be able to release it now that we have the chips themselves."

"And the shirt," Rebecca said, clearly enjoying herself. "With the hole that will match your scrap."

Mary Sue, Joan thought, and wondered whether Fred had asked Ralph about her yet.

She heard the telephone then, in the kitchen. Andrew unfolded himself from his seat on the rug and picked it up on the second ring. "For you, Mom," he said, stretching the long cord all the way to the end of the sofa.

"Excuse me," she told Fred and Rebecca, who continued their gleeful postmortem without seeming to notice. She sat down and tucked her feet under her. It was Alex, asking her to remind the orchestra members to show up at ten o'clock Saturday morning to finish the rehearsal that had been interrupted by the discovery of Mary Sue's body.

"Oh, Alex, we told them on Wednesday," she objected. "And it's Friday night. I have better things to do than call sixty people when most of them will be out anyway." I can hardly believe I said that out loud, she thought, but I'm glad.

It didn't faze Alex. "Then call the section leaders and ask them to notify the others," she said firmly. "I don't

trust them to remember anything they heard that night.''
She had a point. Joan sighed.

"All right, I'll try. But I'm not going to be able to reach
them all.''

"Sure you will!" Alex boomed cheerfully, now that
she'd won. Shades of Mary Sue. "Wake them up tomorrow if you need to. I'll see you then,'' she said, and hung
up.

Across the room, Rebecca and Fred were still congrat-
ulating each other on quick reflexes and fine detective
work. For a few moments Joan just sat there, basking in
their glow. Then she dug out her orchestra personnel list.
She'd make the most important calls now, but leave the
rest till morning. She started with Eddie.

Oh, well, she comforted herself after the eighth ring, at
least we got to finish the Ives on Wednesday. Just when she
was about to hang up, a tired-sounding woman's voice
answered. Eddie's mother, as it turned out, had been
counting on his help hauling trash to the dump and com-
post to the garden after he delivered his Saturday morning papers.

"This won't take long,'' Joan assured her. "It doesn't
start till ten, and he'll be home well before noon.''

"He'd better be,'' the voice whined in her ear. Little kids
were yelling in the background, and a baby was tuning up
much closer to the phone. Poor mother.

Poor Eddie. How had he ever learned to play so beautifully in the first place? Resolving to be extra nice to him
from now on, Joan reached for the personnel list and dialed again. This time she reached a machine. The voice was
that of a young man.

"You picked a bad time to call. We're (a) in the shower,
(b) getting drunk, or (c) not interested in talking to you
anyway. Please leave a short message for Scott, Julie,

Dave, or Sara after the long beep. If we're in a good mood, we might call you back.'' She held the receiver away from her ear, waiting for the beep.

It was going to be a long evening. She hoped Fred would still be there when she finished with the leaders. But he wasn't. Ten minutes later, his pocket beeper sounded, and he took off. She barely had a chance to say good-bye.

HE WAS ALREADY at the inn when she arrived at nine the next morning to be sure everything was ready for the orchestra.

"Sorry I had to duck out like that," he said, taking the box of music from her.

"I was the one who ducked out," she told him. "You and Rebecca were having such a good time, I hated to interrupt. I spent most of the next hour on the phone."

"Nothing wrong, I hope?" He followed her through brilliant color to the ballroom, where stands and chairs stood more or less in order.

"Just work. Alex was afraid people wouldn't show up this morning—you can put that down anywhere, thanks." She waved at the box.

"So you were elected." He set it on the floor.

"I survived." It sounded harsh in her own ears. She softened it. "I'm fine, Fred. Is there anything I ought to know to tell the orchestra folks this morning? Anywhere off-limits to them?"

"No, I don't think so."

"Not even the room where we found Mary Sue?"

"We're finished in there. The damaged quilts we took to the lab are safe in our evidence room. We didn't find anything in them, though, and believe me, we looked. Just the stuffing—polyester in some, cotton in others, an old quilt in one. About all we really learned was that the threads were cut, not broken. That means the quilts were cut off the poles, not ripped down.''

"So much for our theories."

"Not necessarily. If the killer found what he was looking for in one of the quilts, it wouldn't be there now for us to find."

"So you do think it was a man." Not Kitty, after all. Ralph?

"Huh?"

"You said, 'what *he* was looking for.' ''

"Doesn't signify. I can't get used to he/she and his/her."

Before yesterday, at least, Rebecca would have given him a lecture on why it mattered to try. Maybe not now. Joan figured he already knew. He wasn't going to volunteer anything, that was plain.

Leaving the music downstairs, she went up to check what Eddie would have to deal with. Edna's undamaged quilts, hanging up now, and the sunshine streaming through two narrow windows overpowered her gloomy memories of the room. The fateful sadiron—or a dead ringer for it—sat on the potbellied stove in the middle of the room. On sudden impulse, Joan opened the iron door and peered into the firebox. A little heap of ashes inside suggested to her why the room might have been warm on Tuesday. Had someone found the will then and burned it? No, not then, when the whole family was gathered together. Besides, what good would that do? There had to be an original at the lawyer's office. It was bound to surface sooner or later.

Leaving the room, she almost bumped into a white-gloved woman with blue hair.

"Are you my relief?" the woman asked.

"No, I'm here for the orchestra," Joan said. "Sorry."

"This is positively the last time I'll agree to sit," said the woman, opening out a folding chair that had been leaning against the wall. "They've left me stuck up here for hours and hours!"

"How long do you have to stay?" It wasn't quite ten o'clock. Surely the inn hadn't opened before nine.

"Until I'm relieved. But you know how far it is to the little girls' room down the street. I think I'll die if someone doesn't come soon."

"I'll remind the lady at the door," said Joan. "Would that help?"

"Bless you, child," said Blue Hair. And then, as if remembering her duties, "Did you get your ballot?"

"Ballot?"

"To vote for your favorite quilt."

"I don't know anything about quilts."

"That doesn't matter. The judges have made their selections. Now it's our turn. Just write down the one you like best."

"My daughter entered the show—I'd have to vote for hers."

"Oh? Which one is it?"

"The double sleeping bag downstairs. You know, the one of Adam and Eve making love."

The woman blushed to her blue roots. "I don't believe I saw that one."

Just as well, if hearing about it embarrasses you. Joan accepted a ballot and escaped down the stairs, past a quilt made entirely of blue-jeans pockets and an all-white one with stitching so close and fine that it drew lines of tiny shadows. She didn't pause to look at it. Remembering her promise, instead, she reported the hall sitter's distress to the dragon at the door.

"Oh, that Ethel," the woman said, and ran a pencil down a duty roster. "She's signed up to sit until noon. Honestly, I sometimes think she's more trouble than she is help. Don't worry about Ethel—I'll find someone to send up to her."

In the ballroom, the first members of the orchestra were already setting up. Joan found Eddie and sent him upstairs.

"We don't absolutely have to run through the Ives again, but see if you can bear to play in the same room as before."

"Do I have to?"

"No, Eddie, we could try out another one. But this one is easiest for Alex and me, and she liked the sound the other night. Take a look—it's different in the sunshine."

"She won't be there?" He wasn't really asking. More like telling himself.

"No, of course not. Go on, scoot." He did, and came back looking much relieved.

The rehearsal went smoothly. Joan particularly enjoyed several pieces by William Billings—the earliest American composer she had ever played. They did run straight through the Ives after all, less for Eddie, whose five notes were simple, than for the flutes, whose growing confusion took real concentration to pull off. They ended, as they would on Sunday, with Hoagy Carmichael's "Stardust," a crowd pleaser anywhere, but especially in his native Indiana. Even Alex found no fault today and dismissed the orchestra at half past eleven. Nice for Eddie's mother, Joan thought. Maybe even for Eddie, if he drags his feet a little. But Eddie took off at a lope.

No one hung around to look at the quilts. There was little ordinary conversation. People stopped talking abruptly when Joan passed by, as if they'd been caught gossiping about her family.

John Hocking was the exception.

"What have they found out?" he asked her. No need to say about what.

"I haven't heard much." And it was true.

"It's a damn shame."

"Yeah."

"I see your daughter sold her quilt." He nodded at the blank white wall next to the viola section. Joan's mouth dropped open. Rebecca hadn't said a word. But why had she come so far to showcase her concept, only to let a purchaser take her sleeping bag before the show even started? Didn't people usually put a SOLD sign on the tag and wait? There wasn't so much as a red dot here. She shook her head.

"I didn't know."

At home she congratulated Rebecca on her sale.

"My what?"

"Your sleeping bag. You know. It's gone."

"You mean to tell me someone bought it and took it away?" Rebecca's face paled. "Already?"

"You didn't know."

"Of course I didn't know. I never heard of such a thing, and I certainly didn't agree to it. I'm going right over there." Pulling on her pea jacket, she ran out the front door.

WHEN REBECCA came back half an hour later, Fred Lundquist was with her, looking grim.

"What's wrong?" Joan asked. But she already knew from their faces.

"It's not sold, Mom. It's just not there."

"Oh, no!"

"No one at the quilt show knew anything about it. They take the money and keep track of who owns what, but they didn't take any money for my quilt. According to their records, it's still on the wall."

"I'm sorry, Joan." Fred was holding his notebook. "When did you first miss it?"

"I didn't, actually. It was John Hocking."

"Who's that?" He was scribbling.

"My stand partner. He's on your orchestra list from the other night. He's the one who spotted Rebecca's name the first time."

"Wednesday?"

"Right."

"And when you got there today, it was gone?"

"I suppose so. I didn't miss it until after we played. That's when John told me. I don't know when he noticed. He wasn't in any hurry to tell me—he thought it was sold."

"So when did you actually see it last?"

"During rehearsal Wednesday. Afterwards, in all the excitement, I didn't notice."

And then it came to her. While she and Fred had wrapped the lights, she'd been facing the wall John Hocking had reached out to stroke. A plain white wall in a room vibrating with color. She tried again. "You remember that night, when we were sitting downstairs wrapping stand lights?"

"Yeah."

"We were sitting in the first violin section, and I was facing the wall Rebecca's quilt was on. Only it wasn't. The wall looked fine—just a wall. I didn't think a thing about it. But earlier, when we were rehearsing—it feels like a year ago—I was sitting right by that wall, and Rebecca's quilt was on it."

"You sure you've got the right wall?"

"Fred! That's like asking a shortstop whether he's sure the batter didn't run to third instead of first. The firsts never move, no matter where the conductor puts the rest of us."

"Sorry."

"But I can't imagine how someone could take it with all those cops around."

"Maybe it disappeared before you found the body."

"No," she said. "I'm sure it was there when I went upstairs for the Ives. John was close enough to touch it. I don't see how it could have left before he did. He would have noticed—that quilt was hard to miss."

"The colors?"

"The sex." She watched his eyebrows climb. "I'm sure Rebecca told you that she quilted Adam and Eve into a double sleeping bag. She may not have told you that you can't help seeing that they're making a good start on the human race."

Rebecca dug into her duffel bag and handed him a photograph. Fred looked, grinned, and tucked it into his breast pocket. "I can't promise miracles," he said. "But I owe you one."

He went out the door and immediately stuck his head back in.

"I forgot to tell you, Joan—Ralph has an alibi. Snarr's called him at half past eleven that night to pick up a body up in Indianapolis. By the time he got up there, filled out the paperwork, brought the body here, embalmed it, and prepared it for viewing the next morning, Gil Snarr says there's no way he could even have come over to the inn, much less killed Mary Sue and laid her out, too. Odds are, he was still up in Indy."

Joan felt instant relief. As if it makes any difference, she thought. Rebecca's here, and they've caught Ralph. But I can't help it. You must have known I'd feel like this or you wouldn't have told me.

"Thanks, Fred," she said. And he was gone.

"Now there's a man." Rebecca stood at the window, watching him drive off. "Why are you wasting your time with that other character?"

"This character doesn't seem particularly interested. I think he's been burned. Anyway, Rebecca, I'm not looking for a man."

"Uh-huh."

Rebecca pushing a man at her? And a cop, at that.

TWENTY-TWO

Lawyer's Puzzle

HOW HAD SOMEONE smuggled a double sleeping bag past the officers on duty at the Sagamore Inn Wednesday night? Fred's mind boggled. Diamonds, now, he thought, or those computer chips—anything small could easily have ridden out in an instrument case. And we weren't searching people for weapons. But something this big—he tried unsuccessfully to imagine it folded along the back of a string bass. The case would be about right, he thought, but you'd have to leave the instrument behind.

On the way back to the inn, he swung by the station and filled Johnny Ketcham in. Then he walked across the street to clear the cobwebs out of his head.

Even with Ralph alibied, Rebecca's missing quilt was already playing hob with his theory about Mary Sue's murder. If the murder and the theft were related, a possibility he had to consider, then it no longer made sense to look only at the family. At least they both happened at night, he thought. That narrows it down some. I'd hate to have to consider everyone who was at the inn this week.

Inside, he spotted Officer Root standing at the rear of a quilt-filled room in which a lecturer was holding forth to an attentive crowd.

"In a reaction to the plastic culture of this century, women and men have taken joy in rediscovering this ancient craft, in creating something with roots in the past and a flexibility that stretches into the future, in expressing themselves in useful objects of great beauty, in enhancing the visual and tactile qualities of earth-grown fabrics even as they experiment with others.''

Fred caught Root's eye when the lecturer took a breath. He jerked his head and she came out to him.

"Yes, sir?"

"You like this kind of thing?'' He gestured around them.

"I like the quilts—I used to sleep under quilts my grandma made before I was born. I'm not so sure about the lectures.''

"Then you won't mind missing the rest of this one.''

She stiffened. "No, sir. I'm on duty, sir.''

"All right, Root, take it easy. I'm not chewing you out. We're missing a quilt from the show, and I want you to work on it.''

"Yes, sir.'' She relaxed a little.

"We don't know much. We do have a good description of the quilt, and a color photo.'' He handed it over. "It's a sleeping bag, really. I don't think you'll have any problem with identity.''

"No, sir.'' Looking at the picture in her hand, she grinned broadly. "Doesn't look as if they're getting much sleep, does it, sir?''

"Loosen up a little, Root. Let's save some of the sirs for formal occasions, okay?'' He smiled at her, pretty sure she wouldn't take it wrong.

"Okay.'' She didn't sound harassed.

"This sleeping bag seems to have disappeared Wednesday night while we were all here and before the last of the orchestra people left. The one person we can count out is the manager. But anyone else who was here at that time is a possible. What I'd like you to do is find out just how many people that includes. I'll work with Sergeant Ketcham on the orchestra—he has that list. You connect with the quilt-show people about the workers and anyone else who may still have been here from earlier in the day."

"And the kids?"

"I don't think so. Seems to me they arrived after Mrs. Spencer took off, and she remembers seeing the blank wall where this quilt had been hanging. But you can check that."

"I don't need to. I brought them in here when they arrived, and I remember seeing her leave before then."

"You knew her?"

"No, sir. But her picture was in the paper the next day, and—well, some of us recognized you, too."

"I don't doubt it," he said dryly, knowing the gossips in the department. "The people here at the inn know the quilt is missing. They'll be very cooperative. We're not trying to establish any certainties here. See how much you can get out of them. Ask to check their written records, but don't assume that everyone in the building made it into the log."

"Yes, sir. Anything else?"

"Maybe later. Report back to me."

"Mind if I ask something?"

"Go ahead."

"Why are you giving this to me instead of a detective?"

"They're working on the murder, for one, and I like the way you think. What kind of cop do you want to be, Root?"

Her eyes shone. "A detective, sir."

"Okay, then, go to it. Keep your eyes and ears open."

"Thank you, sir." She took off.

He wondered suddenly whether Catherine's name would turn up on the list. According to Joan, Catherine had been catering at the inn on Tuesday, and they'd had some kind of run-in. Might she have been cleaning up Wednesday night? And if she'd seen the name "Spencer" on a quilt, might she have put two and two together and taken it out of spite? The caterer would have had no problem carrying out anything that would fit in a garbage bag—maybe even with garbage on top. He hated to think it of her, but at least it would mean there wasn't a connection between the theft of Rebecca's quilt and Mary Sue's death.

Even considering the possibility reassured him that he was more than likely still on the right track in focusing on the family for the murder. The detectives on duty today were making the rounds of the law offices in town by phone, looking for the lawyer who had drawn up Edna Ellett's will—if there was one—who knew how long ago? For a town no bigger than it was, Oliver had an amazing number of lawyers. He checked his watch. After one now, and not a word.

As if in response, his beeper called him back to the station. When he checked out at the front door, Officer Root was listening to an animated account from Saturday's dragon.

Johnny Ketcham met him in the detective squad room.

"I think we've found it," he said. "We'll have to go over, but it sounds right."

"What does?"

"Well, we ran out of active lawyers an hour ago. Then Terry had the bright idea of looking up retired attorneys. This was an old woman, after all."

"Good thinking." He nodded at Chuck Terry, tall, black, and in his early thirties, whose work was as steady as his demeanor ordinarily was cool. Today, though, he was smiling broadly.

"No luck at first," Ketcham said. "But it put us on the right track. Our next step was to go after dead lawyers."

"I wouldn't touch that one—"

"Yeah. But we got the names from the bar association, and started calling widows. And I think we've found him."

"Yeah?"

"A Mrs. Cox just told Chuck she read about the murder and remembered old Mrs. Ellett as one of her late husband's clients."

"How would she know?"

"She used to be his office secretary—says she's still got files in her basement."

"Get a warrant for the will."

"We won't need it, Lieutenant," Terry said.

"Glad to hear it. But I want this squeaky clean."

"Yes, sir."

"And call me when you've got it. I'd like to be in on this."

THE LATE Mr. Cox had lived in a neighborhood of old money and understated elegance. But the woman who opened the door wore diamonds on both hands and fine lines where her eyebrows should have been.

"Mrs. Cox?" Fred showed her his badge. "Detective Lieutenant Lundquist."

"Come in, please." They filed into a large hallway, with a cherry table along one wall and a walnut staircase rising along the other.

"You spoke to Detective Terry on the phone, and this is Sergeant Ketcham."

"Yes." They didn't shake hands. Instead, turning to the table, she picked up a legal file folder. "After we hung up I went downstairs to see whether we still had the Ellett file, and we did. I say 'we,' but since Sterling's death there's been no one but me. He had a solo practice."

"So you just kept the files?" Ketcham asked.

"No. I wrote to all his clients, asking where to send the documents we were keeping for them—to John Duke, the young man who bought Sterling's practice, or wherever else they chose. Most people have responded by now. In a few more weeks I'll notify the ones who haven't that their files are being transferred to John's office. I'll be awfully glad to get them out of here."

"I can imagine," Fred said. He eyed the file with "Edna Ellett" neatly printed on the tab. Mrs. Cox reached inside it, slid out a few pages neatly bound in a black folder, and handed the folder to him. He looked inside just long enough to read the words "Last Will and Testament of Edna Ellett." Pay dirt.

"I've prepared a receipt for your signature." Whipping out a pen, she handed him a slip of paper with "Received from Susan Cox, conformed copy of Last Will and Testament of Edna Ellett, deceased," typed on it, and the date. Fred leaned over the cherry table to sign it. She opened the file and laid the receipt on top of what appeared to be the letter she had described.

"Thanks. Now no one will ever look at it. But if I didn't have it, sure as anything the family would squawk. You know how it goes."

"Sure."

She closed the file, preserving the confidentiality of a dead woman. They thanked her and left with what Fred fervently hoped would shed some light on the murder of Edna Ellett's daughter.

In the car, with Terry at the wheel, he opened the folder and flipped to the last page to check the date. The will had been signed three years earlier. He didn't recognize the name of one witness, but the other was Susan Cox.

"That's convenient," he said aloud.

"What's that?" Ketcham and Terry asked simultaneously.

"Mrs. Cox witnessed the will. We won't have to track people down if things get sticky."

They nodded. Fred flipped back to the first pages. There was no mention of a husband—she must have written a new will after being widowed. After the usual paragraphs about outstanding bills and funeral expenses, she left her estate "to my three dear children, Alice Ellett Franklin, Mary Sue Ellett, and Leon Ellett, in equal shares; or to the survivor(s), in equal shares, should one or more of them predecease me, after the following specific bequests are paid."

It was a short list. She left five thousand to her church and five hundred to the Senior Citizens' Center—Joan would put that to good use. To Katherine (Kitty) Graf—aha—"my first cousin once removed, who is like a daughter to me, and who will have earned much more by her devoted care, I leave the sum of Ten Thousand Dollars($10,000), my furnished house, and the lot on which it stands." The rest of her personal effects she left to her children and Kitty, "who will, I am confident, have no difficulty arriving at an equitable distribution of the same." Oh, murder.

Then came all the "ifs." If all her children died before she did, their shares would go to Kitty. If Kitty died first, her bequest would go into the pot for the three children. If all four of them died first, Harold Franklin would benefit, "if he is married to my daughter Alice at the time of her death." As a last resort, she had named a number of charities.

Having scanned the will quickly, Fred began reading aloud.

When he came to the house, Ketcham gave a low whistle. "You think that'll hold up in court?"

"As recent as it is, and if people can testify that she was in her right mind, it ought to."

"I hear old Mrs. Ellett was out of it at the end," Terry said. "My Auntie Ruth said it was a real shame." In Oliver, Fred thought, everybody's Auntie Ruth would know.

"I heard that, too," Ketcham said. "But she was sharp when I was a boy running through that house. Question is, when did she lose it?"

"Yeah," Fred said. "But who's going to challenge this? They've all got plenty to lose."

"Leon won't see it that way," Ketcham said. "He's been counting on at least a third of the estate. With Mary Sue dying after her mother and Kitty inheriting too, he'll come out short."

"Leon will get his," Fred told him. "Mary Sue left everything to him and Alice."

"Not the old house. And I expect Alice will have a hard time seeing anyone else living in her mother's house."

"I wonder whether Kitty knew."

"I asked Mrs. Cox if anyone else had been inquiring about Mrs. Ellett," Terry put in, turning at the post office. "She said not."

"Then she probably didn't know," Fred said. "She worried enough to ask a lawyer, but she didn't find the right one."

"What do we do with it now?" Ketcham asked. "The lawyer's dead."

"Notify her executor."

"The will probably says 'personal representative,'" Ketcham said. "Who'd she name?"

Fred flipped another page. Personal representative—Ketcham was right. "Mary Sue." Who better? "Alice is next, and then Kitty. Leon's not even an alternate." The old lady—or her lawyer—didn't trust her son any more than Joan did.

"So it's Alice. Her husband will have a lot to say, if I read that marriage right."

Fred had to agree. "Let's swing by the house and see who's there."

EVERYONE WAS THERE, sitting in the living room. Kitty, acting more like a maid than a member of the family, showed them in and would have left them, but Fred asked her to stay.

"This concerns you."

"Me?" She stood uncertainly on the Chinese rug.

"All of you, really." He looked at the others.

"You've found who killed Mary Sue!" cried Alice, and Leon jumped up.

"No, not yet."

"What, then?" Leon boomed.

"We've just spoken to Susan Cox." No reaction from any of them. "The widow of Sterling Cox."

"Yes?" said Alice.

"Do you know, had your mother heard from either of those people in the past several months?"

Alice shrugged. "I wouldn't know. Kitty?"

Kitty looked blank. "It's possible. I'd been taking care of Edna's mail for some time, but then she got so bad, even before the flu hit. I tried to catch anything that looked really urgent. The rest had to wait." She pointed to an open rolltop desk at the far end of the room, piled high. "If you mean a letter, it could be in that stack."

"Who is this Cox, anyway?" León demanded. "What's this all about?"

"Was. He's dead. Sterling Cox was your mother's lawyer."

"Oh, my God," Harold said almost reverently. "They've found the will."

TWENTY-THREE

All Kinds

"I STILL CAN'T BELIEVE your sleeping bag is gone. I loved it. And two thousand dollars—that's a lot of money." Joan was warming leftover vegetable soup while Rebecca set out plates and drinks for lunch.

"I haven't actually sold one for that much yet. This is only the third one I've made. The other two sold so fast in New York that I decided I must have priced them too low."

"You really expect to get two whole thousand for one quilt?" Joan found it hard to believe.

"There's only one way to find out—after all, I can always come back down. They're individually designed—no two alike. You could probably see that I don't do a lot of detailed quilting. New York doesn't care about that, and it makes a big difference in my labor. But I didn't expect to sell this one here, or win anything for it—and I was right. The judges were awfully conservative."

Then why did you come? Joan thought, hoping she knew. Still, Rebecca was taking her loss amazingly well.

"You seem awfully calm."

"It's a front. But I'm a fast worker. I'm not out a lot of time—mostly the materials. What I'm really marketing is the design, you know, and that's safe in my head. At least you got to see it. I'm glad."

Joan glowed. "Maybe Fred will find it."

"I wouldn't count on it." Twirling a dark curl around her finger, Rebecca was silent for a few moments. Then she looked up as if nothing had ever gone wrong. "How about going with me this afternoon?"

"This afternoon?" Long years of motherhood had left Joan cautious about saying yes without at least checking the facts.

"There's a panel discussion on historical quilts. I'm trying to learn all I can while I'm here."

"Sure, I'll come. The final proofs of the program ought to be back from the printer today—I wanted to check the orchestra part, though it's too late to fix much of anything."

"At least you'll have something to read if the panel is deadly dull." Rebecca grinned at her.

They made short work of lunch, arriving at the inn a few minutes early. A new poster near the door invited them to buy raffle tickets for the orchestra quilt and gave directions to the ballroom, where it could be seen.

"Let's go check how it turned out," Rebecca said. They found it hanging from the balcony behind the brass section, reaching almost to the floor. It would make a splendid backdrop for the orchestra, Joan had to admit to herself. In this setting she could see what Rebecca had meant about the colors and textures.

Rebecca located the border she had quilted near the trombones. "I'm kind of proud of this work, Mom," she said. "It took some self-control not to quilt as well as I know how."

"*Not* to—?" She wasn't making sense.

"Look." Rebecca pointed, careful not to touch the fabric. "Here's where I connected to what the old lady had already done. I can make smaller stitches than hers. Not that these are bad—she was no slouch. They say she was terrific when she was younger. Anyhow, I held back because I wanted my stitches to blend in with hers, not stick out. See? Here, down by the edge, I worked down to my littlest ones, but I made the change gradually, over a couple of inches, so it wouldn't detract from the overall effect.''

At first Joan didn't see. All the lines of stitching looked the same. Then Rebecca pointed to a place where the stitches on the border suddenly were much longer than the others and the border lacked the puffy effect of the rest of the quilt.

''Here's where Kitty couldn't quilt well enough to match her stitches to the old lady's,'' Rebecca said, and Joan remembered watching Kitty make those long, flat stitches. ''It's too bad.''

Joan doubted that anyone but Rebecca would ever notice much beside the instruments and color, but she nodded. Then she remembered the large all-white quilt she'd passed on the stairs that morning, with nothing decorating it but the quilting stitches themselves. Rebecca would appreciate that one, she thought, and she started toward it. Two women coming down the stairs were arguing with enough heat that one of them bumped her and didn't so much as look back.

''I still say they should never have let it in the front door.''

''Get down off your high horse, Edie. It's just a joke.''

''A mighty poor one.'' Edie's indignation trailed off as she went into the next room.

Joan climbed the stairs wondering what could have provoked such an outburst.

''Come on up,'' she called down to her daughter. ''There's something I want to show you.''

''Is that where—?''

"No. Come look at this." At first she could see only the familiar scalloped shape of a Double Wedding Ring quilt and what looked like the rings. Without any colored patches, they seemed somehow incomplete. Then she saw that the effect was intentional. The quilting stitches imitated the patchwork, but the interlocking symbols of eternal love were broken where they should have been linked. In the center, a tired-looking woman had thrown her apron into the air and an angry-looking man was being kissed by a young thing shaped like a Barbie doll. The man and woman were leaning hard away from each other, pulling on a strange, lumpy-looking rope. Looking closer, she realized that they were playing tug-of-war with a rope made of small children. In the four corners of the quilt were a cupid with no arrows, a broken heart, a judge wielding a gavel, and a house split in jagged halves.

Now Rebecca was beside her, reading the label. "It's called Divorce. It's a cartoon! As beautifully quilted as it is, it must have taken her months! Can you imagine spending all that time and effort on anger?"

Joan shook her head, rejoicing that Rebecca's own bitterness seemed to have faded. "What a waste. But you know me—I wouldn't have the patience for all those tiny stitches anyway."

Rebecca laughed. "Not to mention the skill. This one's more your speed." She pointed to the machine-stitched blue-jeans quilt Joan had noticed before, on which every square featured a real hip pocket, some holding scaled-down bandannas. Joan laughed.

They made their way back downstairs to a lecture room crowded with more of Bud Snarr's chairs. The fragile sofas and chairs that were its usual furnishings had been pushed against the walls to make room.

Now the panel members took their seats at a skirted table behind which even the most modest woman would be
able to concentrate on what she was saying instead of having to worry whether her knees were together.

The introductions began. Joan immediately lost the
names and wondered why they couldn't put signs in front
of the people. She retained the bare bones: a tall bean pole
of a woman had worked on the Indiana Quilt Project, a
short, dumpy one on the Kentucky Quilt Project, and a
woman wearing a badge and a ruffled shirtwaist that Joan
suspected of being attached to a long skirt behind the table was a member of the Alcorn County Historical Society. The Oliver College Fine Arts Department was
represented by a young man with a beard.

They began by speaking, first separately and then together, on the importance of preserving quilts, both for
their own sake as objects of beauty and as fragile cultural
artifacts.

"It's a crying shame how many are ruined," the Indiana woman said. "There are simple things you can do to
preserve the quilts you have. *Never* store quilts in plastic,
for instance, or in mothballs. And keep them clean."

Listening to her tips for cleaning a quilt ("pick a warm
sunny day. fill the tub with cool water first, use pure
soap—never detergents or Woolite on cotton quilts—rinse
gently four times, squeeze the water out without letting its
weight pull on the quilt, roll it in mattress pads, lay a sheet
outdoors on flat ground, and lay the quilt on it to dry"),
Joan knew she could never tell such a person that she threw
Grandma Zimmerman's quilts in the washing machine and
dryer with the sheets and towels.

She wanted to cry out, "What about sleeping under
them? What about using them for the purpose for which
they were made? What's wrong with that?" From her

childhood she remembered waking on a cold Michigan morning with the comforting weight of many quilts on her body, and the airy feel of a summer quilt on a warm summer night. When they finally wore out, her matter-of-fact mother had used old quilts in ways that would horrify these people. She had even laid one with holes in it on the floor as a drop cloth. It had, Joan remembered, absorbed the paint spatters beautifully instead of passing them back to shoes, as plastic ones did.

She tuned in better when they argued for documenting the history of the quilter whenever possible.

"People who collect old quilts do well to determine their provenance, and it's rare that we can learn the identity of the quiltmaker, much less details about her life," said the woman from the historical society. "Few family histories have survived to suggest that even such massive upheavals as the Civil War touched their lives. Many quilts have been passed down in families, usually from mother to daughter, but we're a generation too late to hear the stories."

Women's stories, Joan thought. Women's history. Rebecca was nodding again. I must remember to tell Rebecca about old Rachel Berry. Now there's a Civil War story worth hanging on to, and didn't they say some of Edna's quilts came from her?

Then the panel moved on to some of the exceptions. The Kentucky woman waxed eloquent about the spectacular quilts of Virginia Ivey, and what a coup it had been for Louisville to acquire one—she called it "one of the ten or fifteen greatest quilts in the world"—in the low thirties.

"Am I hearing right?" Joan whispered to Rebecca. "This quilt she says is so great sold for only thirty dollars?"

"Not dollars—*thousands,*" Rebecca whispered back. "And that was years ago. They'd never get it for so little now."

Good Lord. More names flew by. Other heads nodded knowingly at mention of Susan McCord's vines, Harriet Powers's Bible Quilt, the Perkins family, Marie Jane Harlan, Marie Webster's quilt patterns, and Elizabeth Mitchell, "known for her famous Graveyard Quilt."

"Her famous what?" Joan whispered, but this time she didn't have to rely on Rebecca. The Kentucky woman told her all about it.

"In her grief after burying two sons in Ohio between 1831 and 1834, Mrs. Mitchell seems to have become obsessed with death. Or maybe just realistic, given the vicissitudes of country living in those days. In any case, in 1839 she created her one-of-a-kind Graveyard Quilt. Mostly in shades of brown, it would have been an attractive, if somewhat somber, Star of Lemoyne, but in the center she put a graveyard and surrounded it by a neat little picket fence. In the graveyard she quilted thirteen coffin-shaped spaces. Four of them are filled—two with appliqué coffins labeled with the names of her lost sons, and two from a row of twenty-one family coffins waiting inside another fence around the outside of the quilt. Having moved from Ohio to Kentucky, Elizabeth couldn't keep going back to visit her dead boys. Perhaps she was afraid the family would continue on the move and so she prepared a family graveyard that she could always keep near her."

"I'll bet nobody ever slept under that one." Joan whispered, grinning at Rebecca.

As if she had heard, the speaker said, "Oddly enough, this is a well-worn quilt." Rebecca grinned back

The art professor stressed how important it was for quilt-makers to know tradition.

"It's as important as for any other artist. Only with an understanding of the past can you go forward, and quilt-makers must try to move forward if quilting is to be an art form. In our time, people who collect quilts as art already look less at traditional technique and more at the composition and painterly qualities of quilts. But this form is not limited to two dimensions. I can't even imagine what it'll be like in ten or twenty years."

Rebecca beamed.

The woman from the historical society traced the resurgence of quilting in the sixties and seventies to a "reaction to plastic culture and the terrible speed at which we live." The Bicentennial, she said, was little more than a convenient peg on which to hang something that would probably have happened without it. "There's a real need in modern life for a natural rhythm, a turning back to the earth. That's why historical societies are flourishing. We're searching for our roots, and we want to do more than just read about them. We want to experience them firsthand."

The questions and answers began with a lively debate about the best way to date an antique quilt.

"Forget about cottonseeds," said the Indiana woman. "Everybody seems to think that finding cottonseeds in quilt batting means you have a really old one, from before 1792, when the cotton gin was invented. But it doesn't. It's easier to date textiles. If you're lucky enough to have old family photographs, you can often date them by the textiles in the clothing the people are wearing. Still, all a fabric tells you is that a quilt was not made before that fabric was available. Old fabrics are often used in much newer quilts—don't be misled."

Joan quickly bogged down in the technical detail that followed.

"I'll see you later," she told Rebecca, and slipped out to look for a program.

"They're due anytime now," said today's doorkeeper. "Can you wait?"

"Oh, sure," Joan said, and wandered back into the ballroom to reassure herself that everything was still in good order for Sunday. Standing at the conductor's desk, she heard voices that seemed to be coming from directly overhead. The echoes in the building gave what were surely ordinary voices an eerie quality.

This must be how it sounds to Alex when Eddie plays his solo from up there, she thought. But who would be up there today? She climbed the stairs and followed the sound past the hall sitter's chair, now empty. There, in the Ellett room, she found Ruby, the old regular who had jumped to Edna's defense the day they worked on the orchestra quilt, talking with a woman she didn't know. Both wore white gloves and badges.

"She showed it to me once, a long time ago," Ruby was saying. "And I'm telling you, it would've walked off with ever' one of them prizes. Course, they ain't nothin' could hold a candle to Edny's quilting."

"But I thought it was a real old one," the other woman said.

"It was," Ruby said, unfazed by her own non sequitur. "Real old. Edny always was a one for old quilts."

Their white gloves protecting the fabrics, the two women were making their way around the room, turning up the corners to examine the stitching on the back of each quilt.

"Hello, Ruby," Joan said.

"Why, hello, honey," Ruby said. "Ain't these somethin'?"

"Except this one," the other woman said. "I wonder how come they ever hung this poor thing next to all those pretties." Joan recognized the simple patchwork squares that had covered Mary Sue's body. They didn't measure up, even to her uneducated eye.

I'm not going to tell them, she thought. I'm just not.

Ruby had found the label.

"It says Edny give this one to that woman who lived with her," she said.

"Not much of a gift, if you ask me," said the other woman.

Poor Kitty, Joan thought. The one artistic member of the family, she would have appreciated something better. It didn't even have the virtue of being old—fresh from the question-and-answer session, Joan saw that some of the squares were fabrics even she could recognize as synthetic.

A buzz of voices downstairs signaled the end of the session, and Joan went back down to look for Rebecca. Finding her among a group of quilt lovers expressing shock at the news of the missing sleeping bag, she left her there and asked one more time at the door.

"The programs just arrived," said the doorkeeper. "But they're so late, they skipped the final proof. I hope they're all right."

"Me, too," Joan said fervently. She wished people who never bothered to send their information on time didn't get so bent out of shape if their names turned up spelled wrong. Carrying a program back to the ballroom, she pulled her orchestra personnel list out of her jeans pocket and sat down in the empty viola section. She had just started comparing it to the one in the program when a familiar voice boomed across the room.

"Little Joan!"

What on earth? It was indeed Leon Ellett, followed
closely by his sister Alice and her husband. Beyond them
Kitty Graf was bringing up the rear. But why?

Joan kept her seat. She didn't think Leon would grab
her, but remembering the scene at Snarr's, she wouldn't
have put it past him.

"I didn't expect to see you all here today," she said,
marking her place with a finger on the page. "Have you
come for the lectures?" Pretty unlikely, when she thought
about it.

"No," Alice said. "We're hoping someone here can tell
us about Mother's quilts."

"We finally found her will," Leon said. "Turns out they
belong to all of us. So Harold, here, suggested that we try
to get them appraised by one of the experts at the show."

"You're planning to sell them?" Joan asked.

"I don't know what else to do," Alice said. "One way
or the other, we need to come out even."

Leon beamed. Harold merely nodded. Kitty frowned.

"Are you sure they're all here?" Joan asked. "One of
Edna's old friends was talking as if a special old one was
missing."

"Nonsense," Alice said, as if Mary Sue had challenged
her. "We brought them all over ourselves."

TWENTY-FOUR

Seek-No-Further

SUDDENLY, IT ALL made sense. Joan stuffed her list inside her program, and her program in her pocket.

"I'll see you later," she said to the Elletts as casually as she could manage. Conscious of every step she took, she walked to the stairs and down them, called to her daughter, and walked out of the ballroom and out the door. Once outside, she let go and ran across the street without checking to see whether Rebecca was following.

Fred beat Rebecca to the front desk by a hair.

"They told me you sounded urgent," he said, and waited.

"We had it all wrong." Joan was breathing hard. "No one was looking for a will in Edna's quilts."

"No?" He didn't look surprised.

"But money—I think you did find money in one—and you still have it."

"Money?" Rebecca was staring at her. "In a quilt?"

Fred shook his head. "We didn't find anything."

"Yes, you did. You told me. You said there was an old quilt inside one of them."

"Sure."

"And I've just heard an old friend of Edna's say that one of her oldest and best quilts is missing. Fred, do you have any idea what great old quilts can be worth?"

"You really think so?" Rebecca said, and turned to Fred. "Can we see it?"

He spread his hands. "It's just an old quilt. But I'll bring it down." He led them down the long hall, past the coffee and candy machines, through a locked door, and to a nearby room, windowless and empty except for a table and four straight wooden chairs. "I'll be right back. Make yourselves comfortable."

Rebecca laughed. Fred looked embarrassed.

"Sorry." He waved at the room. "You get used to it. Would you like a cup of coffee?"

"No, thanks," Joan said. She was champing at the bit.

"Me either," Rebecca said.

They sat down on the hard chairs. Fred waved and disappeared. Then Rebecca pounced.

"What in the world did you hear?"

"You remember Ruby, the old lady who worked on the orchestra quilt? Ruby said Edna had one that was so great, it would have won all the prizes. She hadn't seen it for years."

Rebecca shrugged. "Maybe it was sold."

"No. Edna loved quilts, and she loved antiques. And I'm sure she wasn't that hard up. She would never have sold it."

"Maybe not. But someone else might have."

"Ohhh." It could have happened, Joan knew, during the months when Edna was too ill to take care of herself, much less her things. "Oh, Rebecca, I hope not."

And then Fred was back, looking down at them over four large evidence bags.

"Let's lay these on the table," he said, opening the first bag. "I'm not sure which one it is." He slid out a new-looking quilt decorated with tulips. The binding had been cut open and the border peeled back several inches to reveal only plain cotton batting inside.

"You did this?" Rebecca asked, her face stony.

"We helped it along. Someone else had already cut the edge enough to look in."

"That doesn't make it right!" Joan knew Rebecca was fighting back angry tears.

"Neither is murder," Fred said quietly. "We do what we have to." Refolding the tulip quilt, he slid it back and opened a second bag.

The second quilt, which even Joan recognized as a Log Cabin pattern, had almost no quilting. Lifting the edge, she could see much older patchwork inside. But instead of the valuable antique she had persuaded herself to expect, she saw a tattered, stained quilt held together by sloppy stitches. She was too disappointed to say a word.

"Too bad," Rebecca said. "It wasn't a bad idea, though, Mom. Just wrong."

"Maybe someone did sell it. Fred, I'm sorry we both-ered you."

"It's no bother." He put the Log Cabin quilt back into its bag.

"But since we're here, would you mind if we took a look at the other two?" Rebecca asked.

"Oh, sure." And he displayed the others, both crisp quilts pieced with many contrasting prints.

"They're all new, did you notice?" she said to Joan. "So you weren't all wrong."

"Come again?" Fred said.

"You thought the killer was trying to find something hidden in one of these quilts?"

"And maybe succeeded."

"These four quilts are all made with modern fabrics. That looks as if the killer thought it had been hidden fairly recently—and knew how to tell new quilts from older ones."

"Kitty would know, wouldn't she?" he asked Joan.

"Probably," she said reluctantly. "I don't know about Leon. And some of the old ladies at the center think Alice doesn't know beans about quilts."

"Maybe I'll go over to the Ellett house and have a little chat."

"We just saw them at the inn," Rebecca volunteered.

"Oh?"

"Seems they've all inherited Edna's quilts," Joan said. "They're hoping to find someone to appraise them."

"Let's go, then," he said. "I'll just return these to the evidence room."

"We'll wait," Rebecca said.

And so they crossed the street together, Rebecca's black curls bouncing as she led the way. Why don't I just go home? Joan wondered. I don't want to live through any more of this. I don't *want* to know who in this family would kill Mary Sue.

She climbed slowly to the room with Edna's quilts—she would try to think of it that way. Dawdling, she made small talk with the afternoon hall sitter. Finally, she went in. Leon, Alice, and Harold were standing near the window with Rebecca.

Over by the fireplace, Fred was speaking to Kitty in a soft, matter-of-fact voice. "Here's what I think," he said. "I think you were afraid you'd be out in the cold when Edna Ellett died. You didn't know whether she had put you in her will—that's what you were trying to find out by visiting lawyers the week before the murder." He paused. Kitty, her eyes wide, didn't say anything. The others, too, kept silent. Joan listened in dismay.

"You knew she hid notes—you even found one in a quilt. Then one day it occurred to you that she might have hidden her will in a quilt. When all her quilts were hanging here, you came back after all the others had left, and you started hunting for it in the ones she had made since you came to live with her. But you didn't know that Mary Sue had come back, too. She walked in on you and caught you in the act—cutting into her mother's quilts. So you killed her."

Kitty erupted.

"I didn't! I never would! Never!" Her voice cracked and broke.

"I don't have proof," he said. "Yet. But I'll get it. Meanwhile, you have the right to remain silent." And he recited the whole Miranda warning, still in that calm voice.

"Oh, sure," she said, her voice strong and sarcastic now. "I just reached up and whacked her. Or do you think Mary Sue waited for me to climb up on a chair?"

Looking at the slender woman whose head scarcely reached Fred's shoulder, Joan remembered seeing Mary Sue standing nose to nose with Leon. Kitty was right, she thought. She would have had a hard time hitting Mary Sue with a sadiron. With a poker, maybe. But the old inn's fireplace was missing all its interesting equipment.

And all the things Fred had been saying to Kitty could apply to Leon, only more so. She couldn't keep quiet another minute.

"Fred, I don't believe it," she heard herself saying. "Kitty was sure she wasn't in Edna's will. Why would she want to find proof that she wasn't? The longer they didn't find it, the longer she could put off having to find a new home." Fred didn't answer.

"But she *was* in it," Leon told her.

"She was?"

Kitty looked at the floor.

"It's true," Alice said. "Mother left Kitty the house and a cash bequest and an equal share with the rest of us in all her personal possessions."

"Including the quilts," said Harold. "That's why we came over here."

Meanwhile, Rebecca had been studying Edna's quilts.

"Here's a new one nobody has cut into yet," she said.

Joan recognized the homely patchwork Ruby and the other woman had been clucking about. Fred went over to Rebecca.

"Is this the only one?" he asked her.

"I think so," she said. "It's certainly the most likely one. All the others look older. Not just from the fabrics, but from the quilting stitches. The very last quilting Edna did was on that orchestra quilt. These stitches are almost as long as those—nothing like her earlier work. You can see how beautifully even and fine they are on a dozen of the others."

"Then let's get someone up here with scissors," he said.

"No!" Kitty cried.

"Now, Kitty," Alice said. "If Mother hid something in there, we need to know what it is."

"No, you don't," Kitty said stubbornly.

"Maybe there's another will," Leon said. You hope, Joan thought.

"Or maybe Mom's right," said Rebecca. "Maybe this thing is hiding the missing quilt. I'll find some scissors." She went out.

"There's no missing quilt," Alice said. You're probably right, Joan thought, sighed, and waited. In what seemed like no time Rebecca was back, with the tall, skinny woman from the Indiana Quilt Project in tow.

"I'm looking forward to these quilts," she said. "I hear it's the first time they've been exhibited anywhere."

"That's right," said Alice. "Mother was very protective of them."

"More like secretive," Leon said.

"But what's this about wanting to cut one up?" the woman asked. "Surely you don't mean it."

"Not cut it up," Alice said. "We just want to look inside it. We'll be careful not to damage it."

The woman looked at the ugly duckling, holding it out and examining the quilting stitches showing through on the backside.

"Oh," she said. "I think you ought to be able to do that. This one would be easy to repair." She pulled a little pair of sharply pointed sewing scissors out of her pocket and held them out.

"No!" Kitty said again.

"I couldn't," Alice said. Leon and Harold shook their heads. Joan put her hands behind her back, and Rebecca just smiled.

"I guess that leaves me," the woman said. "Well, I'm as curious as the next person." She hardly had to stretch to cut the basting threads and release the quilt from the muslin sleeve on the high pole. But then, cradling it, she looked around.

"I need a place to spread it out," she said. "I can't very well lay it on the floor."

Joan remembered how it had looked spread over Mary Sue's body. It wouldn't be the first time, she thought gloomily, and wondered who had hung it up again. But Fred spoke up.

"There's a table and chairs next door." So they all trooped past the hall sitter to the next room.

The quilt project woman slid the tips of the scissors under the seamed edge of the binding, skillfully cutting only the threads that attached it to the edge from which it had been hanging.

"Don't," Kitty whispered, when she quickly nicked several of the sparse lines of running stitches at short intervals. The first threads were just coming loose when Kitty went to pieces, lunging at her and screaming, "Stop it! It's mine! You have no right!"

Startled, the woman stepped back immediately, and the hall sitter stuck her head in. But Fred grabbed Kitty by the shoulders and gestured to the woman to continue while he held Kitty back.

"We have every right," he told them both. "It's evidence found at the scene of a crime. What's in it?"

"Just a little more, and we should be able to see," the woman said, pulling on a thread and peeling back the edge.

"Oh!" Rebecca exclaimed over her shoulder. "It *is* here!"

"What's here?" Alice asked.

"I'm not sure," the quilt project woman said slowly. "But if the rest is anything like this, it's a treasure."

TWENTY-FIVE

Gift of Love

A TREASURE. The dollar signs sparkled in Harold's lenses, and Leon was grinning openly.

"I can't believe it. Burying this in that old thing." Shaking her head, the quilt project woman snipped longer and longer threads to speed up the work. Rebecca, her eyes wide, helped her pull the threads and peel the top back, gradually revealing an all-white quilt that far surpassed anything Joan had ever seen.

"Ohhhh," marveled the hall sitter, clasping her white gloves.

Kitty was sobbing quietly now. Tears streamed down her face. "You have no right," she repeated in a whisper. It sounded like an echo—of what?

"According to the will—" Alice began, but Kitty cut her off.

"It wasn't *in* the will. It was mine!"

"She's right," Joan said. "Look at the label. Edna gave her this quilt—insides and all—before she died." And she knew why the whispered words had echoed. She had heard them first in this very room, through the vibrant Double Wedding Ring quilt now hanging on the wall. It had to be Kitty who had whispered "You have no right" with such passion. But who was the other whisperer? Who had said "I know what she left me"—Alice? Maybe. But how could Alice be so sure? She hadn't visited her mother for more than a year before her death. Who would Edna have thought could talk the hind leg off a mule—Leon? Ahh. The shoe fit. Joan knew Leon's charm all too well. He could probably charm Edna, she thought. But not even Leon could sweet-talk Mary Sue out of anything that mattered. So he killed her to try to get what he wanted—not realizing that it would belong to Kitty after all.

She caught Fred's eye over Kitty's head and pointed to the Double Wedding Ring, hoping he'd remember the rest. He raised a questioning palm.

Now what? It doesn't make sense to suggest a private chat—even as quiet as Kitty is now, he can't very well let go of her. Or can he?

"Fred, we need to talk."

"Go ahead."

"Right here in front of God and everybody?"

Fred just smiled at her. Well, all right.

"You remember I told you about hearing two people whispering up here?" He nodded. "And what they said?" Another nod. "Kitty's saying it again today. The first one had to be Kitty."

"Right."

"And the other one..." She tilted her head toward Leon. But the quilt project woman spoke up.

"Could someone go after the other participants in this afternoon's panel? They really ought to see this quilt *in situ.*"

"In what?" asked the hall sitter.

"You'll do," Fred told her. "Do you know who she means?"

"Yes, I was there."

"Then go get them." The woman hesitated. "And while you're at it, bring up the police officer on duty downstairs."

"Oh, I will, I will." Reassured, she bustled out.

"So it wasn't Kitty who was cutting into the quilts at all," Joan continued doggedly. "She'd never risk damaging this one—she must have known all along it was there. But we know Leon was looking for his mother's will. Maybe he even found it, and when he saw how much less he'd get than the courts would have given him if she'd died intestate, he burned it in the Franklin stove. Then he pretended there wasn't any." Leon shook his head and stared at her with hound-dog eyes.

"I thought you knew me better than that," he said. Joan couldn't meet his eyes. What if she was wrong? After all, Alice and Harold would have had the same motive for destroying Edna's will. Leon turned his back on her. Confused now, she fell silent and watched the table.

Sooner than seemed possible, the white-on-white quilt lay entirely exposed, a wonder of hearts, pineapples, and cornucopias overflowing with apples, cherries, and grapes, all connected by twining grapevines. No longer concerned with protecting its outer covering, the quilt project woman had pulled a pair of clear plastic gloves from her pocket and was now spreading it smoothly on the narrow table and examining it section by section.

"How old would you say it is?" Rebecca folded the outer patchwork down at one end. Its backing protected the white quilt from the table.

"At least a hundred, but probably much older. It's superb."

"Is it a bride's quilt, do you think?"

"Almost certainly. And it comes from a family well enough off that the young woman could devote many hours and many yards of fabric to a white cover that was never intended for much real use. Even so, you can see signs of wear here—and here. All in all, it's remarkably well preserved."

"It's mine," Kitty whispered.

"How very fortunate you are, my dear," the woman said, stroking a padded heart. "Do you know its history? Did it come down in your family?"

How can you ask her that? Joan thought. Haven't you heard a thing? But maybe not—you've been so intent on what you were uncovering.

The rest of the afternoon's speakers arrived then and began poring over every inch of the discovery. Fred stepped back and let them protect it. He posted the uniformed officer—a woman—outside the door and stood quietly just inside it. With no one challenging her claim, Kitty calmed down. She actually seemed to be enjoying the attention her treasure was receiving and the questions the experts were asking her.

"Edna Ellett and my mother were first cousins on the Berry side—my mother was a Berry," she explained. "Old Rachel Berry—the one they tell the war story about—was their great-great-grandmother, our great-great-great-grandmother. She passed it down to Edna, who gave it to me. Edna always said she wanted it to stay in the family." She looked daggers at Alice and Harold.

"This is outrageous!" Alice said. "You must have used undue influence on Mother. Everyone knows she wasn't clear in her mind these last few years."

"She didn't know what she was doing," said Harold.

"She knew exactly what she was doing," Kitty said sharply. "You would have sold it to the highest bidder, and she knew I wouldn't." Joan wondered how many thousands it could bring on the open market.

"You wouldn't?" Alice said. "Just what are you planning to live on?"

"I don't need much. Maybe I'll do for other old people whose families aren't up to it. Edna was always grateful for the least little kindness."

If Mary Sue ever said anything that saccharine it would have been to slam Alice, Joan thought. From Kitty, I believe it. But how were things really between Kitty and Edna? Alice might be right—a grateful old lady would be easy pickings for an unscrupulous caretaker, especially after she was no longer herself. I wish I'd seen more of Edna in those last months. I wonder how long ago she hid this antique. Not at the very last—even quilting that simple patchwork by herself must have taken a long time. Besides, if Rebecca's right about those stitches she's just been taking out, they were better than what Edna was able to do by then. But knowing when she hid it away doesn't tell us when she gave it away. Leon said his mother played her cards close to her chest. Looks as if she trusted Kitty more than she did her own children. Was she right?

Kitty was starting the tale of how Rachel rescued Abner from the pile of corpses. Leon couldn't resist a story, and soon the whole family was adding details as if nothing had happened.

"Wonderful!" said the historical society woman. "I wonder whether this quilt goes back that far. Did Rachel make any others?"

"We don't know that she made this one," Alice said. "But Mother always said several of her old ones came from Rachel."

"This one is special," Rebecca said. "Look at the detail, and the trapunto." She tilted her head to one side to get the full impact of the padding. "Oh, look," she said. "Down here in the border. There's writing in the quilting, very small."

"Does it say Rachel Berry?" Alice asked.

"I can't really see. It looks like a couple of names and a date." Rebecca stepped back, yielding her view to the experts.

"SARAH BERRY, 1805," the Indiana Quilt Project woman read aloud. "I knew it was old, but this is wonderful. No wonder your mother wanted it to stay in the family."

"And the other name?" Alice asked. There was a long pause.

"I don't believe it," said the Indiana woman finally. She held up the corner of the quilt to the raking light. "It's mighty little. You look," she said to the Kentucky woman.

"N. Hanks," the Kentucky woman read. "N. Hanks in 1805? Nancy Hanks? It could be."

"You're talking about Abe Lincoln's mother?" Joan could hardly believe her ears. "This is signed by Abe Lincoln's mother?"

"You're very lucky," the historical society woman said to Kitty. "If this is genuine, it's priceless."

Joan remembered hearing something about a Lincoln letter in the Ellett family. Maybe it wasn't a letter at all, she thought.

"So that's how the Kentucky Berrys ended up with something to do with Lincoln," she said. "It had nothing to do with the war."

"Kentucky Berrys—of course," said the Kentucky woman.

"Then it can't be the right Nancy Hanks," said the Indiana woman.

"Yes, it can," said the Kentucky woman. "She lived with the Berry family in Washington County, Kentucky, before she married Tom Lincoln there in 1806—as I live and breathe, it *is*."

"Not according to Herndon. He said she lived with the Swallows."

They stared at each other. Joan wondered whom they were talking about.

"These days most scholars agree that she grew up with her wealthy Berry cousins in Washington County," the historical society woman said. "Herndon was neither her contemporary nor a scholar—I never did believe him. But even Herndon agrees with everyone else that she excelled at needlework. Now here's a Berry name linked with hers, and the date's right. And people wonder what historical value quilts have!"

"Not to mention its monetary value," said Harold. "We really must ask you to assess that."

"It doesn't matter," Kitty said. "It's mine, and it's not for sale."

"*If* you can prove that Edna really did give it to you before she died," he said. "We have only your word for that."

For once, the Elletts were united.

"That's it," Leon said to Kitty. "It wasn't Mom who hid the Hanks quilt—it was you!"

"You made that patchwork top," Alice said. "You knew no one would want it if it didn't look like much. You gave it to yourself."

TWENTY-SIX

Bull's Eye

IT MADE A certain sense. Kitty had had ample opportunity to slap together an undistinguished top and back and quilt it poorly, so that no one would challenge her claim to Edna's greatest treasure. But why had she bothered to mention Edna at all? If she had just said, "I made this one," no one would have paid any attention to it.

Oh sure, Joan answered herself. And how would she have accounted for the Berry/Hanks quilt when she later "discovered" it? I suppose she could have claimed that it came to her through her own mother, if she really was a Berry. The Elletts haven't questioned the part about her mother—that must be right. So why not do that in the first place? Why this convoluted pretense about a gift from Edna, unless it's not a pretense at all, but the truth?

Around the table the quilt people, apparently oblivious to the confrontation between Kitty and the Elletts, were concerned with establishing the authenticity of the N. Hanks signature.

"Who was Sarah Berry?" asked the Indiana woman. "I never heard of her."

"Sarah was Nancy's best friend," said the Kentucky woman. "Maid of honor at her wedding. Nancy named Abe's older sister Sarah after her."

"Wrong Sarah," said the historical society woman. "That was her cousin Sarah Shipley, who also lived with the Berrys. I think there was a Sarah in the Berry family, but I don't remember anything about her descendants.''

"Maybe she never married.''

"Maybe that's why her wedding quilt stayed with the Berrys.''

"It doesn't have a red-and-green Kentucky binding.''

"Those came later.''

And on and on. Joan's head swam. She wondered what Fred was making of all this as he stood back and let it flow. Rebecca, at first fascinated, soon left the table and came over to her.

"Mom,'' Rebecca said quietly. "You and I know it's not true.''

"Huh?'' What did Rebecca know about Nancy Hanks?

"I'm going to tell Fred that Kitty didn't hide that quilt.''

Her voice was soft, but Fred's antennae must have been out. "What was that?'' he said, and came over to them.

"Kitty didn't hide it,'' Rebecca said. "Only we've just destroyed the evidence.''

"You'd better explain,'' he said.

For the second time that day, Rebecca sped him through a concise explanation of long and short quilting stitches.

"Kitty couldn't possibly have done the work we just pulled out of the patchwork,'' she ended. "Ordinary as it was, it was so far beyond hers that there's no doubt. I can show you her work downstairs.''

Joan nodded. "It's true, Fred. You could ask her.'' And she pointed to the Indiana woman. "She saw the stitches they took out. I'm sure her memory for such things is good enough to make the comparison with what Kitty did on the orchestra quilt. Even I can, and I agree with Rebecca.''

"Let's say you're right,'' he said. "And just for the moment, let's say Kitty's telling the truth and Edna gave it to her. How did it end up here?''

Kitty turned her back on Leon, Alice, and Harold to respond. "They wanted all Edna's quilts in this room. She made that one, so Mary Sue said it belonged here. I tried to keep it home, but she insisted. I didn't know how to say no."

"Did you know what was in it?" Rebecca asked.

Kitty ducked it. "I knew it was her gift to me." Joan and Fred exchanged looks.

"And you didn't plan to cut into it," Joan said.

"No!"

"I believe her, Fred. Why should she come here late at night to cut into something that belonged to her? Look." And Joan pulled the quilt show program out of her pocket. "Not only does it say so on the wall—it's printed in the program notes supplied by Mary Sue, who knew more about her mother's quilts than anyone else in the family. All Kitty had to do was wait until *after* the show, with her right as owner firmly established."

"But you did come back that night, didn't you?" Fred said in that conversational tone. "Or maybe you never left at all. Actually, I'm inclined to think that's more likely."

Kitty stared at him.

"Alice told her old friend Johnny Ketcham that you said you were too wound up to sleep that night and you wanted to walk home alone. She said Leon dropped her and Harold off at her mother's house and drove home alone. It appears that Mary Sue went home to her house but returned for some reason—we know she had keys to the inn. Leon didn't want you and Alice to talk because he knew we'd find out that none of you could alibi the others."

"Yes," Joan said. "And Mary Sue would have let any of them back in."

"It wasn't that way!" Kitty blurted.

"Are you calling me a liar?" Alice demanded.

"No." Kitty was quiet again.

"Maybe Leon went back after he dropped the others off," Joan said. "He arrived about the same time as Mary Sue. She let him in, and—I don't know what."

"He made some excuse to go upstairs," Rebecca said. "Then he started cutting into quilts, the way Mom said. Mary Sue came in and caught him, and he clobbered her."

"He's tall enough," Joan said, not looking at him. That's it! she thought. That's why it must have been Leon. She felt better. "Alice and Harold couldn't reach up there without a ladder. Neither could Kitty."

"Mmm-hmm," Fred said. "But you're forgetting somebody."

"Who?"

"Mary Sue was tall enough."

"Mary Sue is dead!" Joan felt silly as soon as she'd said it. She was sure her cheeks were red. Fred smiled at her. "Oh," she said. "I see what you mean. But why?"

"Maybe the will," he said. "But I doubt it. Mary Sue was the one member of her family who was interested in quilts, the one person likely to know—or at least suspect—what was in this one."

"And she'd know old from new," Joan said.

Fred nodded. "Suppose she started in systematically checking the new ones for the Hanks quilt, one after the other. She had no luck with the first three, but no problems, either. Then she attacked the right one. Like this." And he pulled out a pocket knife and advanced on the table, shoving his way roughly between the Kentucky woman and the Indiana woman. They gasped.

"No!" Kitty screamed, and ran at him. She threw herself at his six-foot Swedish frame and hammered his back with both fists, for all the world like little Amahl in *Amahl and the Night Visitors,* Joan thought, desperately pound-

ing the guard who grabbed his mother when she went for
the gold. The uniformed officer pulled Kitty off Fred and
restrained her arms. Trembling, she sat down in a heap.

Joan was glad that Fred didn't overreact to what was,
after all, an assault on a police officer. He asked Kitty
softly, "Is that how it was with Mary Sue?"

"It was mine! It was all I had! She had no right!" She
was shaking.

"So you killed her."

No! Joan thought.

"I never meant to kill her," Kitty said in a small voice,
looking at the floor.

Kitty, no! I don't want to hear this.

"Why didn't you just yell at her to stop?" Fred's voice
was gentle. Kitty looked up at him, her eyes filled with
tears.

"I was going to. That's why I stayed. But when I saw her
with those scissors, the iron jumped off the stove into my
hand. I hit her once and then I couldn't stop hitting her.
Then she stopped moving."

"Katherine Graf, you're under arrest for the murder of
Mary Sue Ellett." Fred gestured to the uniformed officer,
who handcuffed her unresisting wrists in front of her.
"You have the right to remain silent. If you choose to give
up that right—"

"I know. You already told me my rights."

"Did you understand them? Including your right to
have an attorney present during questioning?"

"Yes. But I don't want one. He might shut me up, like
Leon. It's such a relief to talk about it."

TWENTY-SEVEN

Bars

FRED HAD EXPECTED shock and opposition, but after the scene at the inn not even Joan, for all her staunch championing of Kitty Graf, had objected to her arrest. With Kitty's lack of resistance, he and Root had simply walked her across the street to the station. They'd booked her, and now she was waiting with Root in the interrogation room where he had shown Joan and Rebecca the damaged quilts only a little while earlier.

Johnny Ketcham met him in the hall and peered through the glass window at the slender figure in the wooden chair.

"She confess?"

"Yeah," Fred said. "I saw it coming from her first reaction when they cut into her quilt. Then she let a couple of things slip. A little ham acting, and she was begging to tell me all about it. She had the keys to the inn in her pocket. Come on in before she changes her mind. The video's running." He opened the door.

Kitty, her wrists free again, was sitting in the stuffy room with a cup of black coffee cooling on the table in front of her. Root rose to leave, but Fred motioned her to stay. He reminded Kitty that she had been advised of her rights and had chosen to waive the right to an attorney during her interrogation. "Unless you've changed your mind?"

"No."

"Then tell us in your own words what happened a week ago Tuesday night."

She sat silent for a long moment. He was on the verge of prompting her when she began. At first she spoke to the table, her voice so soft that he hoped the video would catch it. He didn't want to risk distracting her by asking her to speak up.

"You know I was over at the inn helping hang Edna's quilts on Tuesday." She glanced up. Fred nodded. "We finished sometime after midnight."

"We?"

"Mary Sue, Leon, and Alice. And Harold, Alice's husband. You already know what happened then."

"Suppose you just tell it the way it happened."

"Mary Sue went home to her house. Leon offered the rest of us a ride to Edna's house, but I said I wanted to walk. Only I didn't go home. I'd found a door I could prop open—there aren't any alarms in that old building. So I put a stick in it and pretended to leave. When they were all gone, I went back in."

"Why? What did you expect would happen?"

"I didn't know what would happen. I just knew I'd gotten talked into leaving the biggest thing Edna had ever given me in that building, and I didn't trust it or Mary Sue as far as I could throw her."

"You thought she'd come back?"

"I didn't think—I was just scared."

"Why especially Mary Sue?"

For the first time she met his eyes. "You knew her?"

"Yes."

"Then you knew her mother had it right. She *could* talk the hind leg off a mule. She was the one who made me take the quilt there. She was the only one in the family who knew anything about quilts—or their value. I was just hired help to her—not that Alice cared or I trusted Leon to do all that he promised. But I knew that if Mary Sue had any idea what was inside that quilt, she'd never let me keep it. She was the most likely person to miss it from Edna's collection. And it was all I had from Edna. All I had, period, as far as I knew. I didn't know what was in her will—that's why I was so scared."

"So you killed her."

"No! I didn't go there to kill anyone. I just wanted to keep an eye on it." Fred didn't buy it.

"You planned to stay up all night? And all the other nights?" She was silent. "How? How were you going to do that?" Finally, she shrugged.

"I was going to cut it down and take it home—steal my own property. I figured nobody would get too excited about a mediocre quilt. I could make a little fuss, and they wouldn't suspect that I had it."

"But you didn't?"

She shrugged again. "I couldn't reach it. Maybe if I'd had long shears—I don't know. But all I had were Edna's little sewing scissors, and I couldn't come close to cutting it down."

Fred and Ketcham exchanged glances. Ketcham spoke up.

"What did they look like?"

"Like little storks. I don't know what happened to them. When I got home I couldn't find them."

"So then?" Fred said.

"Then I knew I'd just have to wait it out. But I fell asleep. I'd sat up with Edna a lot while she was so sick, and then there were all those people in her house—I didn't know yet that it was going to be my house." She shook her head wonderingly. "If I'd known..."

They waited, but she didn't finish her thought.

"Did the kids come by?"

"Once. But I was hiding behind a bed, watching the door. They didn't come in—just waved a flashlight around and went on. They were laughing and carrying on. Nice kids."

Fred doubted that the mayor would appreciate a good review of his daughter's behavior from this source.

"I'd been sleeping a little while—I don't know how long—when I saw light. And there was Mary Sue, cutting into Edna's quilts as if she had a right to. I suppose she did, in a way. But then I saw she was about to start in on mine. And—well, I told you what happened then."

"Tell me again."

"I never meant to kill her! I didn't start out to. I ran at her to stop her, but when I went past the stove, my hand brushed the old iron that was on it. I didn't decide to pick it up. But then I was hitting her with it, and I just couldn't stop." She ran down suddenly.

"The kids didn't come in?" Ketcham asked.

"No. Mary Sue didn't make a sound, not even when she toppled over. I don't think she ever knew what hit her. And she landed on quilts." Kitty shuddered.

"On her back?"

"No, on her face. I hit her on the back of the head—and the top." Fred nodded. If he'd had any doubts, they were gone.

"Then what did you do?"

"I picked up her scissors and keys. I took the scissors home and put them in Edna's sewing box. I was afraid to get rid of the keys. I wasn't sure I would have to get back in."

"And the iron?"

"Funny—I don't remember seeing it again. Maybe I couldn't. I couldn't bear to leave her all bent over on her face like that— I didn't hate her. So I turned her over and laid her out. And I covered her."

"With what?"

"My quilt. But I didn't want it to touch her. Not because she was dead—she didn't bleed at all. I was afraid her lipstick could leak through the patchwork onto the good quilt. So I went hunting for the plastic bags we'd brought them over in. Just to protect it, you know."

"Why did you leave your quilt there? Why not take it home the way you first planned?"

"Everything was different. It wasn't just a plain quilt anymore. I knew that if anything disappeared out of that room you'd look harder for it because Mary Sue was dead. It was listed in the program, you know. Besides, now it was as safe there as anywhere. At the end of the show, I could still just claim it in the ordinary way and take it home. No one would want it who didn't know what was inside."

"Could you prove it was yours?"

"No, and that's what scared me. Edna knew what the rest of them would do if they ever found out I had it. When I went to live with her, back when her mind was clear, she told me she was going to have her lawyer draw up a paper when she wrote her will. But I never found out whether she did it or not."

That's why you were looking for the lawyer who drew up Edna's will. Fred kicked himself for limiting the warrant to the will.

"And then? After you covered her?"

"I turned off the light, walked home, and went to bed."

"What time did she die?"

"I don't know. I got home by two."

Fred sat quietly, but she had run down.

"Anything else you want to tell us?" he asked finally.

"That's all."

TWENTY-EIGHT

Wandering Foot

KITTY'S ARREST and sudden departure left the inn in turmoil. The wonderful Berry quilt—signed by someone who just might have become the mother of Abraham Lincoln—had been borne off as evidence. A quilt show worker had produced a plain white pillowcase and helped fold it with care after the quilt project women extracted a promise that it would be treated as the fragile antique that it was. Then they were gone.

"What will happen to her?" Rebecca asked Joan, who had been wondering just that.

"I don't know."

"I feel kind of sorry for her."

"I know. I keep thinking that if that iron hadn't been there, she wouldn't have hurt Mary Sue any worse than she hurt Fred just now."

Alice was visibly shaken.

"Don't worry, old girl," Leon told her. "She won't get a penny of Mom's estate now."

"Is that true?" Rebecca asked Joan.

"I don't know the law, but I don't see why it should be."

"You can't profit from your own crime," Harold answered. "But Alice, that won't apply to your mother's estate, or, for that matter, to the quilt. They belonged to Kitty before she killed Mary Sue. Nothing changes that."

"No," Alice said. "If they were taken from her, we'd be the ones profiting from Mary Sue's crime. She was the one trying to take what was Kitty's."

Alice, you're okay, Joan thought. I wonder whether Edna's bequest is enough to pay for a good lawyer. What if Kitty has to sell that quilt?

AT SUPPER they filled Andrew in. He pumped them for more. Finally he asked something Joan couldn't answer.

"You said Kitty was too short to cut down those quilts, and she said she'd have to climb on a chair to kill Mary Sue. Is that what she did?"

"I don't know. It doesn't seem likely. I just don't know."

Rebecca leaned forward suddenly. "You remember Dad's favorite riddle? The one Rabbi Plaut taught him?"

"What's green and hangs on the wall and whistles?" Andrew said promptly.

"Right. And the answer?"

"A red herring."

"But that's not green," she deadpanned.

"So? You can paint it green."

"But it doesn't hang on the wall."

"Is there a law that says you can't hang it on the wall?"

"Well, no. But"—triumphantly—"it doesn't whistle."

"No," he said sadly. "It doesn't whistle." They laughed, not because it made sense or was new, but because it didn't and was old.

"So," Andrew said. "What does that have to do with anything?"

"I just got to thinking. What was short and cutting quilts? Mary Sue Ellett."

"But Mary Sue wasn't short."

"Not if she was cutting the quilts down."

"But she *was* cutting them down."

"Not when she was cutting into them."

"Don't get picky," Andrew said.

"I mean it. Think a minute. She didn't stand there slitting them and peeking into the top edge from an angle that would be impossible even for her. First she cut them down. We watched a tall person do that to one—and then take it into the next room so she could spread it out on a table to look inside. But Mary Sue didn't have a table. Where did you and Eddie find the quilts, Mom?"

"On the floor—oh! She was cutting into them on the floor. She must have bent over them."

"Maybe. Or knelt on the floor. I always cut out my fabric on my hands and knees."

"So what's short and cutting *into* quilts works," Andrew said. "I wonder if they've figured that out yet."

"I wouldn't be surprised," Joan said. "But there's no hurry now. I can tell Fred anytime."

She half-expected to hear from him, but the phone was silent that night. When she woke Sunday morning she found Andrew and Rebecca eating breakfast. Rebecca's duffel bag was standing by the kitchen door.

"You're leaving? So soon?" Just when I'm truly glad you came?

"It's not soon. I've got to get back to work tomorrow. I can catch a plane tonight, after your concert."

"If you'll let me drive her to the airport," Andrew said.

"Of course. I'll come, too."

WITH ALL WORRIES about random murders set to rest, Mayor Deckard cut a red ribbon and declared the quilt show open at one o'clock. At two-thirty, Alex mounted the podium.

The crowd, rather than walking by as expected, stayed put to tap its feet to the lively numbers and stand quietly for the Ives. Joan held her breath when Eddie played, but he didn't falter, and the effect was all Alex could have hoped for. The response was enthusiastic, and Alex tossed in "The Stars and Stripes Forever" as an encore. Now people were lining up to buy chances on the instrumental quilt, as they would be able to do all week.

Joan watched them, her viola tucked safely under her bow arm. Andrew and Rebecca were suddenly beside her.

"Congratulations, Mom!" Andrew said.

"I didn't expect this little town to have such a good orchestra!" Rebecca looked as if she meant it.

"Thanks. It really went all right, didn't it?" She had felt good about the music, but their approval delighted her.

"More than all right," Rebecca said. "That piece with the trumpet upstairs would have given me the shivers even if I hadn't known."

"Too bad you couldn't advertise it, Mom—the murder probably doubled the attendance as it was." Andrew grinned. Then he peered at the empty wall to Joan's left. "Say, Bec, is this where—?" She nodded. "They've left your sign up, anyway."

"For all the good that does." She shrugged. "Guess I'll go home and start over again." Home? Joan thought. Well, sure. Oliver was never home to Rebecca—I didn't realize until this minute that it feels like home to me today. I can even recognize some of the faces.

A friendly one was advancing on them now.

"Fred!" Rebecca cried. Joan smiled. And I wondered what she'd think of a cop.

He shook hands with Andrew and put one arm around Rebecca's shoulders before hugging Joan with the other. "I'm sorry I couldn't see you last night," he said, his eyes crinkling down at her. "I was afraid to call you by the time we were done with Kitty—I knew you had to play today." She smiled up at him, feeling content.

"Thanks, Fred. It was okay. I already knew more than I read in the paper this morning."

"Yeah. But without you two there wouldn't have been anything to read."

Rebecca beamed. Cops one, cynics nothing.

"Maybe not yet," Joan said. "But you were sure all along—just not for the right reasons. You would have gotten there eventually."

"Mmm," he said. "Eventually's a long time, especially when the mayor's breathing down the chief's neck. I'm grateful. Now if I could just find Rebecca's quilt."

"Oh, Fred, it's not your fault!" Rebecca said. Cops two, cynics weakening fast.

"No, just my job." On cue, his beeper beeped. He let go of Rebecca to turn it off. "I'd better check it out. You'll be here for a little bit yet?"

"Oh, sure," Joan said. "It takes a while to roll up those lights. And Fred, if you see the new person from Snarr's, send him back to me. They want these chairs out of here ASAP." He nodded, gave her a little squeeze, and took off through the crowd.

"Well, now," Annie Jordan said from behind Joan. "I wouldn't call it moving fast, but you do arrive, don't you?" For once, she was without her knitting, but she hadn't left her tongue at home.

"Have a heart, Annie—at least in front of my kids."

"They shock easy?" Annie's old eyes sparkled.

"Oh, you." But Joan enjoyed Annie's teasing. Putting her viola and bow in their case, she started on her end-of-concert duties—collecting music, unplugging stand lights, and rolling up the cords for storage. Andrew took off with Rebecca, who was taking a last look at the quilts.

Too bad about Rebecca's, Joan thought. I wish that hadn't happened. But I'm proud of how she's responding. Now where's that carton for the lights?

At first she took it for granted that she had simply forgotten where she'd put it. But as the players dispersed, the instrument cases behind which the carton could have been hiding gradually disappeared. A few minutes later, standing in an almost empty room, she knew she had a problem and decided to ask the nearest hall sitter. She was glad to recognize Ethel, the blue-haired woman who had been so desperate for relief on Saturday morning.

"A cardboard box about this big?" Ethel said. "Yes, I saw it. But it looked kind of messy sitting out in the ballroom, so I put it in a press in one of the rooms upstairs. I'll show you."

In a what? Joan wondered, but she followed Ethel, as grateful for her help as she was annoyed at her interference. At the top of the stairs Ethel turned into the first room and walked to the back. With her white gloves she gently lifted the corner of a pink-and-white sawtooth quilt and held it away from two pale green wooden doors set into the wall.

"There," she said. "Just open it." Joan pulled on the handles and the doors opened, revealing shelves—evidently a press was a linen closet. Sure enough, her grubby cardboard box was resting on what was probably an antique quilt that belonged to the inn when it wasn't hosting a show. Then she caught her breath. The pinkish-brown quilt was altogether too lumpy for an antique. It couldn't be—could it? She reached in and swept the shelf bare. The empty carton flew out, and Adam and Eve tumbled to the floor in all their passion.

"Stop!" Ethel cried. "Someone will see!" Her face aflame, she was trying to scoop up the naked figures. And Joan remembered watching her blush when she heard about the sleeping bag.

"No, Ethel," she said. "You can't keep hiding my daughter's quilt."

Now Ethel's eyes opened wide and she stared at Joan's long black skirt and pumps—concert dress.

"Not much like blue jeans," Joan said. "But you'd never have brought me up here if you'd recognized me first, would you?"

"Please don't turn me in," Ethel begged. "I wasn't stealing it, I swear I wasn't. I was protecting it!"

"That's a lot of bull, and you know it."

"You didn't see the letter!"

"What letter?" Joan couldn't help it.

"When I came in that day, there was a horrible obscene letter fastened to it. Someone was threatening to do vile things to Adam and Eve. So I hid them."

"Where's the letter? Why didn't you show it to the police? This place is crawling with them, or hadn't you noticed?" Joan didn't believe in any such letter. Ethel didn't answer. "There wasn't any letter, was there?" Still no answer.

"That's what I thought."

"I burned it." So soft, she could hardly hear it.

"You *what?*"

"I couldn't show that letter to a man, I just couldn't. So I burned it in the Franklin stove. You almost walked in on me, don't you remember?" And Joan did remember. I found the ashes. Then I saw Ethel in the hall. I thought for a minute I'd found the missing will, and so I missed finding Rebecca's quilt.

"What are you going to do to me?" Ethel asked.

"If it were up to me, I'd probably hang you from the nearest rafter. But I don't know what my daughter will say."

"Thank you! Oh, thank you!"

Ethel's gratitude embarrassed Joan. She gathered Rebecca's sleeping bag into her arms. "Come on, Ethel. Let's go tell Rebecca."

It was a joyful reunion in spite of Ethel's tears. Rebecca insisted on telling Fred, but agreed not to sign a complaint so long as Ethel was barred from ever working another quilt show. They found him at the front door and left him there to work it out.

"Now I can go home happy," Rebecca told Joan, as they stood watching Adam and Eve being restored to their place on the wall. This time it sounded right. "And there's still the viewers' choice award. I wonder whether Carolyn got hers back in time to be in the running for that, at least."

"You mean Carolyn Ryrie?" asked the worker hanging the quilt.

"Yes, do you know her?"

"We just hung her quilt—they gave it a special judges' award. I think she's still up front celebrating."

"I'll be right back!" And Rebecca took off running.

Fred came back to admire the wall.

"Fred Lundquist, what have you been up to?" Annie Jordan greeted him. "You've got a smile on your face like a wave on a slop bucket." He pulled his face straight, but his eyes kept dancing.

"A little private business, Annie."

Just then the doorkeeper crossed the ballroom and stuck a red dot on Rebecca's label. For a moment, Joan was dumbfounded. Then she wheeled on Fred.

"Fred, you didn't!"

"Well," he said. "You never know when you'll need a sleeping bag made for two."